PH

‖‖‖‖‖‖‖‖‖‖‖‖‖‖‖‖‖‖‖‖‖
P9-DDR-878

RANDOM HOUSE
LARGE PRINT

PLUM LUCKY

Also by Janet Evanovich
available from Random House Large Print

Twelve Sharp
Eleven on Top
Ten Big Ones
To the Nines
Hard Eight
Seven Up
Plum Lovin'

Full House
Full Tilt
Full Speed

Visions of Sugar Plums
Lean Mean Thirteen

PLUM LUCKY

——————

Janet Evanovich

R A N D O M   H O U S E
L A R G E   P R I N T

LP
MYS
EVANO

This is a work of fiction. Names, characters, places, and incidents either are the product of the author's imagination or are used fictitiously. Any resemblance to actual persons, living or dead, events, or locales is entirely coincidental.

Copyright © 2007 by Evanovich, Inc.

All rights reserved.
Published in the United States of America by Random House Large Print in association with St. Martin's Press, New York.
Distributed by Random House, Inc., New York.

The Library of Congress has established a Cataloging-in-Publication record for this title.

ISBN: 978-0-7393-2776-0

www.randomhouse.com/largeprint

FIRST LARGE PRINT EDITION

10 9 8 7 6 5 4 3 2 1

This Large Print edition published in accord with the standards of the N.A.V.H.

Jacket design by Jerry Todd

I'd like to acknowledge the invaluable assistance of Alex Evanovich, Peter Evanovich, and my St. Martin's Press editor and friend, SuperJen Enderlin.

PLUM LUCKY

1

My mother and grandmother raised me to be a good girl, and I have no problem with the **girl** part. I like men, malls, and carbs. Not necessarily in that order. The **good** part has been spotty. I don't steal cars or sniff glue, but I've had a lot of impure thoughts. And I've acted on a bunch of them. Not limited to, but including, snooping through a guy's closet in search of his underwear. On the surface, this doesn't sound like a majorly hot experience, but this was no ordinary guy, and I couldn't find any underwear.

My mother and my Grandma Mazur are **really** good. They pray every day and go to church regularly. I have good intentions, but religion, for me, is like tennis. I play an excellent mental game, and in my mind's eye I look terrific in the little white skirt, but the reality is I never actually get onto the court.

It's usually when I'm in the shower that I think of things spiritual and mystical and wonder about the unknown. Like, is there life after death? And just what, exactly, is collagen? And suppose Wonder Woman actually exists. If she was discreet, you might not know, right?

Today is St. Patrick's Day, and when I was in the shower this morning, my thoughts were about luck. How does it work? Why are some people flat-out lucky and others not so lucky? Virgil said fortune favors the bold. Okay, so I read that on the stall door in the ladies' room of the multiplex last week, and I don't personally know Virgil, but I like his thinking. Still, there has to be something else going on besides being bold. Things we can't comprehend.

My name is Stephanie Plum, and I try to leave the incomprehensible in the shower. Life is tough enough without walking around all day wondering why God invented cellulite. I'm a skip tracer for my cousin Vinnie's bail bonds agency in Trenton, New Jersey, and I spend my day hunting felons who are hiding in attics. It was a little after nine A.M. and I was on the sidewalk in front of the bonds office with my sidekick, Lula.

"You're a holiday shirker," Lula said. "Every time a holiday comes up, you don't do your part. Here it is St. Patrick's Day and you don't have no green on you. You're lucky there's no holiday police because they'd haul your boney behind off to the shirker's dungeon."

"I don't own anything green." Okay, an olive drab T-shirt, but it was dirty.

"I own lots of green. I look good in it,"

Lula said. "But then I look good in all colors. Maybe not brown on account of it blends with my skin tone. Brown's too much of a good thing on me."

Lula's borderline too much of a good thing in lots of ways. It isn't exactly that Lula is fat; it's more that she's too short for her weight and her clothes are too small for the volume of flesh she carries. Her attitude is Jersey times ten, and today her hair was candy-apple red. She was packed into shamrock-green animal-print stretch pants, a matching green sequin-encrusted stretchy top, and spike-heeled dark green suede ankle boots. Lula was a hooker before she took the job at the bonds office, and I was guessing this outfit was left over from the St. Patrick's Day fantasy collection.

Truth is, I sometimes feel a little boring and incredibly pale when I'm with Lula. I'm of Hungarian and Italian descent, and my complexion is more Eastern European than Mediterranean. I have shoulder-length, unexceptional, curly brown hair, blue eyes, and a nice nose that I inherited from the Mazur side of the family. I was in my usual jeans and sneakers and long-sleeved T-shirt that carried the Rangers hockey team logo. The temperature was in the fifties, and Lula and I were bundled into hooded sweatshirts. Lula's sweatshirt said KISS ME I'M PRETENDING I'M IRISH, and mine was gray with a small chocolate ice cream stain on the cuff.

Lula and I were on our way to get a Lucky Clucky Shake at Cluck-in-a-Bucket, and Lula was rooting through her purse, trying to find her car keys.

"I know I got those keys in here some-where," Lula said, pulling stuff out of her purse, piling everything onto the hood of her car. Gum, lip balm, stun gun, cell phone, a forty-caliber nickel-plated Glock,

Tic Tacs, a can of Mace, a personal-mood candle, a flashlight, handcuffs, a screwdriver, nail polish, the pearl-handled Derringer she got as a Valentine's Day present from her honey, Tank, a musical bottle opener, a roll of toilet paper, Rolaids . . .

"A screwdriver?" I asked her.

"You never know when you'll need one. You'd be surprised what you could do with a screwdriver. I got extra-strength cherry-scented condoms in here, too. 'Cause you never know when Tank might be needing some emergency quality time."

Lula found her key, we piled into her red Firebird, and she motored away from the curb. She turned off Hamilton Avenue onto Columbus Avenue, and we both gaped at the gray-haired, wiry little old lady half a block away. The woman was dressed in white tennis shoes, bright green stretch pants, and a gray wool jacket. She had a white bakery bag in one hand and the strap to a large canvas duffel bag in the other. And she was struggling to drag the duffel bag down the sidewalk.

Lula squinted through the windshield. "That's either Kermit the Frog or your granny."

Grandma Mazur's lived with my parents ever since my Grandpa Harry went to the big trans-fat farm in the sky. Grandma was a closet free spirit for the first seventy years of her life. She kicked the door open when my grandpa died, and now nobody can get her back in. Personally, I think she's great . . . but then I don't have to live with her.

A car wheeled around the corner and rocked to a stop alongside Grandma.

"Don't look like there's anybody driving that car," Lula said. "I don't see no head."

The driver's side door opened, and a little man jumped out. He was slim, with curly, short-cropped gray hair, and he was wearing green slacks.

"Look at that," Lula said. "Granny's wearing green and the little tiny man's wearing green. Everybody's wearing green except you. Don't you feel like a party pooper?"

The little man was talking to Grandma, and Grandma wasn't looking happy with him. Grandma started inching away, and the little man snatched the strap of the duffel bag and yanked it out of Grandma's hand. Grandma roundhoused the man on the side of his head with her big black purse, and he dropped to his knees.

"She handles herself real good, considering she's so old and rickety," Lula said.

Grandma hit the little man again. He grabbed her, and the two of them went down to the ground, locked together, rolling around kicking and slapping.

I wrenched the door open, swung out of the Firebird, and waded into the mix. I pulled the little man off Grandma and held him at arm's length.

He squirmed and grunted and flailed his arms. "Let me go!" he yelled, his voice pinched from the exertion. "Do you have any idea who I am?"

"Are you okay?" I asked Grandma.

"Of course I'm okay," Grandma said. "I was winning, too. Didn't it look like I was winning?"

Lula clattered over in her high-heeled boots, got Grandma under the armpits, and hoisted her to her feet.

"When I grow up, I wanna be just like you," Lula said to Grandma.

I swung my attention back to the little man, but he was gone. His car door slammed shut, the engine caught, and the car sped down the street.

"Sneaky little bugger," Lula said. "One minute you had a hold of him, and then next thing he's driving away."

"He wanted my bag," Grandma said. "Can you imagine? He said it was his, so I asked him to prove it. And that's when he tried to run off with it."

I looked down at the bag. "What's in it?"

"None of your beeswax."

"What's in the bakery bag?"

"Jelly doughnuts."

"I wouldn't mind a jelly doughnut," Lula said. "A jelly doughnut would go real good with the Lucky Clucky Shake."

"I love them shakes," Grandma said. "I'll share my doughnuts if you take me for a shake, but you gotta leave my duffel bag alone. No one's allowed to snoop in my duffel bag."

"You don't got a body in there, do you?" Lula wanted to know. "I don't like carrying dead guys around in my Firebird. Messes with the feng shui."

"I couldn't fit a body in here," Grandma said. "It's too little for a body."

"It could be a leprechaun body," Lula said. "It's St. Patrick's Day. If you bagged a leprechaun, you could make him take you to his pot of gold."

"I don't know. I hear you gotta be careful of them leprechauns. I hear they're tricky," Grandma said. "Anyways, I haven't got a leprechaun."

The day after St. Patrick's Day, I woke up next to Joe Morelli, my almost always boyfriend. Morelli's a Trenton cop, and he makes me look like an amateur when it comes to the impure thoughts. Not that he's kinky or weird. More that he's frighteningly healthy. He has wavy black hair, expressive brown eyes, a perpetual five o'clock shadow, an eagle tattoo from his navy days, and a tightly muscled, entirely edible body. He's recently become moderately domesticated, having inherited a small house from his Aunt Rose.

Commitment issues and a strong sense

of self-preservation keep us from permanently cohabitating. Genuine affection
and the impure thoughts bring Morelli to
my bed when our schedules allow inter-
section. I knew from the amount of sun-
light streaming into my bedroom that
Morelli had overslept. I turned to look at
the clock, and Morelli came awake.

"I'm late," he said.

"Gee, that's too bad," I told him. "I had
big plans for this morning."

"Such as?"

"I was going to do things to you that
don't even have names. Really hot things."

Morelli smiled at me. "I might be able
to find a few minutes. . . ."

"You would need more than a few minutes for what I have in mind. It could go
on for hours."

Morelli blew out a sigh and rolled out
of bed. "I don't have hours. And I've been
with you long enough to know when
you're yanking my chain."

"You doubt my intentions?"

"Cupcake, my best shot at morning sex is to tackle you while you're still sleeping. Once you're awake, all you can think about is coffee."

"Not true." Sometimes I thought about pancakes and doughnuts.

Morelli's big, orange, shaggy-haired dog climbed onto the bed and settled into the spot Morelli had vacated.

"I was supposed to be at a briefing ten minutes ago," Morelli said. "If you take Bob out to do his thing, I can jump in the shower, meet you in the parking lot, and only miss the first half of the meeting."

Five minutes later, I handed Bob over to Morelli and watched his SUV chug away. I returned to the building, took the elevator back to my second-floor apartment, let myself in, and scuffed into the kitchen. I started coffee brewing, and my phone rang.

"Your grandmother is missing," my

mother said. "She was gone when I got up this morning. She left a note that said she was hitting the open road. I don't know what that means."

"Maybe she went to a diner with one of her friends. Or maybe she walked up to the bakery."

"It's been hours, and she's not back. And I called all her friends. No one's seen her."

Okay, so I had to admit it was a little worrisome. Especially since she'd had the mysterious duffel bag yesterday and had been attacked by the little man in the green pants. Seemed far-fetched that there would be a connection, but the possibility made my stomach feel squishy.

"This is your grandmother we're talking about," my mother said. "She could be on the side of the road hitchhiking a ride to Vegas. You find people, right? That's what you do for a living. Find your grandmother."

"I'm a bounty hunter. I'm not a magician. I can't just conjure up Grandma."

"You're all I've got," my mother said. "Come over and look for clues. I've got maple link sausages. I've got coffee cake and scrambled eggs."

"Deal," I said. "Give me ten minutes."

I hung up, turned around, and bumped into a big guy. I shrieked and jumped back.

"Chill," he said, reaching out for me, drawing me close for a friendly kiss on the top of the head. "You just about broke my eardrum. You need to learn to relax."

"Diesel!"

"Yeah. Did you miss me?"

"No."

"That's a fib," he said. "Do I smell coffee?"

Diesel drops into my life every now and then. Actually, this visit makes it only three times, but it seems like more. He's solid muscle, gorgeous, and scruffy, and he smells like everything a woman wants . . . sex and fresh-baked cookies and a hint of Christmas. Okay, I know that's an odd combination, but it works for Diesel. Maybe because he's not entirely normal . . . but then, who is? He has unruly sandy blond hair and assessing brown eyes. He smiles a lot, and he's pushy and rude and inexplicably charming. And he can do things ordinary men can't do. At least, that's the story he tells.

"What are you doing here?" I asked him.

"I'm looking for someone. You don't mind if I hang out here for a couple days, do you?"

"Yes!"

He glanced at my coat. "Are you going somewhere?"

"I'm going to my mother's for breakfast."

"I'm in."

I blew out a sigh, grabbed my purse and car keys, and we trooped out of my apart-

ment and down the hall. Mrs. Finley from
3D was already in the elevator when we
entered. She sucked in some air and
pressed herself against the wall.

"It's okay," I said to her. "He's harmless."

"Hah," Diesel said.

Diesel was wearing an outfit that
looked like it belonged in the street-
person edition of **GQ**. Jeans with a rip in
the knee, dusty shit-kicker boots, a T-shirt
advertising Corona beer, a ratty gray
unzipped sweatshirt over the shirt. Two
days of beard. Hair that looked like he'd
styled it with an eggbeater. Not that I
should judge. I wasn't exactly looking like
a suburban sex goddess. My hair was
uncombed, I had my feet shoved into
Ugg knockoffs, and I had a winter coat
buttoned over a pair of Morelli's sweat-
pants and a flannel pajama top imprinted
with duckies.

We all scooted out of the elevator, and

Diesel followed me to my car. I was driving a Chevy Monte Carlo clunker that I'd gotten on the cheap because it didn't go in reverse.

"So, Mr. Magic," I said to Diesel, "what can you do with cars?"

"I can drive 'em."

"Can you fix them?"

"I can change a tire."

I filed that away in case I needed a tire changed, wrenched the door open, and rammed myself behind the wheel.

My parents live in the Burg, short for the Chambersburg section of Trenton. Houses and aspirations are modest, but meals are large. My mother dumped a mess of scrambled eggs and over a pound of breakfast sausages onto Diesel's plate. "I got up this morning, and she was gone," my mother said. **"Poof."**

Diesel didn't look too concerned. I was

guessing in his world, **poof, and you're gone** wasn't all that unusual.

"Where did you find the note?" I asked my mother.

"On the kitchen table."

I ate my last piece of sausage. "Last time she disappeared, we found her camped out in line, waiting to buy tickets to the Stones concert."

"I have your father driving around looking, but so far he hasn't seen her."

My father was retired from the Post Office and now drove a cab part-time. Mostly, he drove the cab to his lodge to play cards with his friends, but sometimes he picked up early-morning fares to the train station.

I drained my coffee cup, pushed back from the table, and went upstairs and looked around Grandma's room. From what I could tell, she'd taken her purse, her gray jacket, her teeth, and the clothes on her back. There was no sign of struggle. No bloodstains. No duffel bag. There was a brochure for Daffy's Hotel and Casino in Atlantic City on her nightstand.

I traipsed back downstairs to the kitchen. "Where's the big bag?"

"What big bag?" my mother wanted to know.

"Grandma had a big bag with her yesterday. It's not in her room."

"I don't know anything about a bag," my mother said.

"Did Grandma just get her social security check?"

"A couple days ago."

So maybe she bought herself some new clothes, stuffed them into the duffel bag, and got herself on an early bus to Daffy's.

Diesel finished his breakfast and stood. "Need help?"

"Are you any good at finding lost grandmothers?"

"Nope. Not my area of expertise."

"What **is** your area of expertise?" I asked him.

Diesel grinned at me.

"Besides that," I said.

"Maybe she just took off for a nooner with the butcher."

My mother gasped. Horrified that Diesel would say such a thing, and doubly horrified because she knew it was a possibility.

"She wouldn't leave in the middle of the night for a nooner."

"If it's any consolation, I don't feel a disturbance in the force," Diesel said. "She wasn't in harm's way when she left the house. Or maybe I'm just feeling mellow after all those sausages and eggs."

Diesel and I have similar jobs. We look for people who have done bad things. Diesel tracks down people with special talents. He refers to them as Unmentionables. I track down people who pretty much have no talent at all. I call them

Fugitives. Whatever name you use for the hunted, the hunter has a job that relies heavily on instinct, and after a while you become tuned in to the force. Okay, so that's kind of Obi-Wan Kenobi, but sometimes you walk into a building and get the creeps and know something ugly is waiting around the corner. My creep-o-meter is good, but Diesel's is better. I suspect Diesel's sensory perception is in the zone ordinarily reserved for were-wolves. Good thing he isn't excessively hairy or I'd have to wonder.

"I'm going back to my apartment to shower and change. And then I'm going to the office," I told Diesel. "Can I drop you somewhere?"

"Yeah. My sources tell me the guy I'm looking for was on Mulberry Street yester-day. I want to look around. Maybe talk to a couple people."

"Is this guy dangerous?"

"Not especially, but the idiots following him are."

"I found a brochure for Daffy's in Grandma's room," I told my mother. "She probably took a seniors' bus to Atlantic City and will be back tonight."

"Omigod," my mother said, making the sign of the cross. "Your grandmother alone in Atlantic City! Anything could happen. You have to go get her."

Ordinarily, I'd think this was a dumb idea, but it was a nice day, and I hadn't been to Atlantic City in ages. It sounded like a perfectly good excuse to take a day off. I had five open cases, but nothing that couldn't wait. And I wouldn't mind putting distance between Diesel and me. Diesel was a complication I didn't need in my life.

An hour later, I was dressed in jeans, a long-sleeved, V-neck sweater, and a sweatshirt. I drove to the bail bonds office, parked at the curb, and walked into the office.

"What's up?" Lula wanted to know. "We gonna go out and catch bad guys today? I'm ready to kick ass. I got ass-kickin' boots on today. I'm wearing a thong two sizes too small, and I'm feeling mean as hell."

Connie Rosolli grimaced. Connie is the office manager, and she's pure Burg Italian American. Her Uncle Lou was wheelman for Two Toes Garibaldi. And it's rumored her Uncle Nunzo helped turn Jimmy Hoffa into a dump truck bumper. Connie's a couple years older than me, a couple inches shorter, and a lot more voluptuous. If Connie's last name was a fruit, it would be Cantaloupe.

"Too much information," Connie said to Lula. "I don't **ever** want to know about your thong." Connie took a file off her desk and handed it to me. "Just came in.

Kenny Brown. Wanted for grand theft auto. Twenty years old."

That meant unless he weighed three hundred pounds, he could run faster than me and was going to be a pain in the ass to catch.

I stuffed the Brown file into my shoulder bag. "Grandma Mazur's hit the road. I think she might be at Daffy's, and I told my mother I'd check on her. Anyone want to tag along?"

"I wouldn't mind going to Atlantic City," Lula said.

"Me, too," Connie said. "I can forward the office calls to my cell phone."

Lula had her bag on her shoulder and her keys in her hand. "I'm driving. I'm not riding to Atlantic City in a car with no reverse."

"I almost never need reverse," I told her.

Connie locked the office, and we all piled into Lula's Firebird.

"What's Granny doing in Atlantic City?" Lula asked.

I buckled myself in. "I'm not certain she **is** in Atlantic City. It's just my best guess. But if she is there, I imagine she's playing the slots."

"I'm telling you, she had a leprechaun in that duffel bag yesterday," Lula said. "And she took him to Atlantic City. It's just the place to take a lucky leprechaun."

"You don't really believe in leprechauns, do you?" Connie asked Lula.

"Who, me? Hell, no," Lula said. "I don't know why I said that. It just come out of my mouth. Everybody knows leprechauns aren't real, right?" Lula turned onto Broad. "Still, there's a lot of talk about them, and that talk has to come from somewhere. Remember that Christmas when Trenton was overrun with elves? If there's elves, there might be leprechauns."

"They weren't elves," I told her. "They were vertically challenged people wearing pointy rubber ears, and they were trucked in from Newark as a marketing strategy for a toy factory."

"I knew that," Lula said. "But some people thought they were elves."

It takes about an hour and a half to get from Trenton to Atlantic City. Forty minutes, if Lula's behind the wheel. It's flat-out highway driving until you get to Pleasantville. After that, it's not all that pleasant since the Jersey poor back up to the Jersey Shore in Atlantic City. We drove past several blocks of hookers and pushers and empty-eyed street kids, and then suddenly the landscape brightened and we were at Daffy's. Lula parked in the garage, and we fixed our makeup, sprayed our hair, and hoofed it through the maze that leads to the casino floor.

"It's going to be hard to spot Grandma Mazur," Connie said. "This place is filled with old people. They bring them in by bus, give them a carton of cigarettes, a ticket to the lunch buffet, and show them how to stick their credit cards in the slot machines."

"Yeah, people in Jersey know how to enjoy old age," Lula said.

It was true. All over the country, we were warehousing old people in nursing homes, feeding them Jell-O. And in Jersey, we were busing them into casinos. Dementia and heart disease didn't slow you down in Jersey.

"You could probably order dialysis off the room service menu here," Lula said. "I tell you, I'm glad I'm gonna spend my golden years in Jersey."

"We'll all go in a different direction and look for Grandma," I said. "We'll keep in touch by cell phone."

I was halfway through a tour of the blackjack tables and my phone rang.

"I found her," Connie said. "She's at the slots, playing poker. Go to the big dog in the middle of the room and turn left."

Daffy's was one of the larger, newer casinos on the Boardwalk. In a misguided effort to out-theme Caesars, the conglomerate owners had chosen to design the casino after the chairman's ten-year-old beagle . . . Daffy. There was a Daffy Doodle bar and a Daffy Delicious restaurant, and Daffy paw prints on the purple-and-gold carpet. The crowning glory was a twenty-foot, two-ton, bronze Daffy that shot laser beams out of its eyes. The dog barked on the hour and was located dead center in the main casino.

I turned left at the big bronze Daffy and found Grandma hunched on her stool in front of a Double Bonus Video Poker machine, concentrating on the combinations. Bells were dinging, lights were flashing, and Grandma kept hitting the PLAY button.

Randy Briggs was standing behind Grandma. He was clutching the duffel bag to his chest, alternately looking around the room and watching Grandma play. Briggs is a forty-something computer geek with thinning sandy blond hair, cynical brown eyes, and all the charm of Attila the Hun. Holding the bag was awkward for Briggs because Briggs is only three feet tall and his arms barely wrapped around the bag. I've known him for a couple years now and wouldn't go so far as to say we're friends. I suppose we have a professional relationship, more or less.

"Hey," I said to him. "What's up?"

"The usual," Briggs said. "What's up with you?"

"Just hanging out." I looked at the duffel bag. "What's in the bag?"

"Money." Briggs cut his eyes to Connie

and Lula. "I've been hired to guard it, so don't anybody get ideas."

"I got ideas," Lula said. "They have to do with sitting on you until you're nothing but a grease spot on the carpet."

Grandma stopped punching the PLAY button and looked around at us. "I'm on a hot streak. Don't get too close or you'll put the whammy on me."

"How much have you won?" I asked her.

"Twelve dollars."

"And how much have you poured into the machine?"

"Don't know," Grandma said. "I'm not keeping track."

"I smell buffet," Lula said. "There's a buffet around here somewhere. What time is it? Is it time for the lunch buffet?"

All around us, seniors were checking out of their machines, getting on their Rascals, and powering up their motorized wheelchairs.

"Look at this," Lula said. "These old people are all gonna beat us to the buffet, and we're gonna have to take leftovers."

"I hate buffets," Briggs said. "I can never reach the good stuff."

"I can reach everything," Lula said. "Every man for himself. Watch out. Coming through. Excuse me."

"I guess it wouldn't hurt to get something to eat," Grandma said. "I've been playing this machine for four hours and my keister is asleep. We gotta get a move on, though, so we don't get behind the feebs with walkers and them portable oxygen tanks. They take forever to get through the line."

The buffet was held in the Bowser Room. We bought our tickets, loaded our plates, and sat down.

"No offense," I said to Briggs, "but you seem like an odd choice to guard the money."

Briggs dug into a pile of shrimp. "What's that supposed to mean? You think I'm not honest? You think I can't be trusted with the money?"

"I think you're not tall."

"Yeah, but I'm mean and ferocious. I'm like a wolverine."

"I want to know more about the money," I said to Grandma. "Where did you get the money?"

"I found it fair and square."

"How much money are we talking about?"

"I don't know exactly. I kept losing my place when I was counting, but I figure it's close to a million."

Everyone stopped eating and looked at Grandma.

"Did you report it to the police?" I asked her.

"I thought about it, but I decided it wasn't police business. I came out of the bakery, and I saw a rainbow. And I was walking home, looking at the rainbow, and I fell over the bag with the money in it."

"And?"

"And it was St. Patrick's Day. Everybody knows if you find a pot of gold at the end of a rainbow on St. Patrick's Day, it's yours."

"That's true," Lula said. "She's got a point."

"I always wanted to see the country, so I took some of the money, and I bought myself an RV," Grandma said. "And this here's my first stop."

"You can't drive," I said to Grandma. "Your license was revoked."

"That's why I hired Randy," Grandma said. "I got a real good deal on the RV because it used to be owned by a little person. The driver's seat is all set up. Soon as I saw it, I thought of Randy. I remembered when you two were on that case with the elves."

"They weren't elves," I told Grandma.

"They were little people trucked in from Newark. And you can't keep this much money."

"I'm not keeping it," Grandma said. "I'm spending it."

"There are rules. You have to report it, and then wait a certain amount of time before it becomes yours. And you probably have to pay taxes."

I couldn't believe I was saying all this. I sounded like my mother.

"That doesn't apply here," Grandma said. "This is lucky money."

"Guess that's why you won the twelve dollars," Lula said.

"You should take some money," Grandma said. "I got plenty." She looked over at Briggs. "Give everyone one of them bundles."

"I don't think that's a good idea," I said to Grandma. "Suppose someone puts in a claim and you have to give the money back?"

"That's the beauty of it," Grandma said. "This here's not ordinary money. It's lucky money. You use it to win more money. So there'll always be money if we need it."

"You've been gambling for four hours and you've only won twelve dollars!"

"It took me a while to get my rhythm, but I'm hot now," Grandma said.

"Are you sure the money doesn't belong to the little man in the green pants?"

"I asked him how much was in the bag, and he didn't know. He's a common thief. He must have seen me find it, and now he wants to steal it."

"He followed us out of the Burg this morning," Briggs said. "Least, I think it was him. It was some little guy in a white Toyota."

I looked around. "Is he here?"

"I haven't seen him," Briggs said. "I lost him when I got into traffic after I turned off the parkway."

"I'm gonna go get some dessert," Grandma said. "And then I'm hitting the slots again."

"I'm skipping dessert and taking my money to the craps table," Lula said.

"Me, too," Connie said. "Only I'm playing blackjack."

Briggs handed the money out and sat tight, using the duffel bag like a booster chair.

2

My phone rang, and I saw my home number appear in the readout.

"It's feeling lonely here," Diesel said. "I'm not getting vibes on you or my target. Where are you?"

"Atlantic City. Grandma's here. She found some money, and she's having an adventure."

"Found?"

"Remember the bag I was searching for in her room? She has it here with her, and it's filled with money. She said she was walking home from the bakery yesterday, and she found it sitting on the curb."

"Green duffel bag with a yellow stripe?"

"Yeah."

"Oh man, what are the chances," Diesel said. "How much money?"

"Around a million."

"I don't suppose there's a little guy with curly gray hair and green pants lurking somewhere?"

"A little guy in green pants attacked Grandma yesterday. And it's possible he followed her out of the Burg this morning."

"His name is Snuggy O'Connor. He's the guy I'm tracking, and the money in that bag is stolen. If you see him, grab him for me, but don't take your eyes off him or he'll evaporate into thin air."

"Really?"

"No. People don't just evaporate. Boy, you'll believe anything."

"You sort of evaporate. One minute, you're standing behind me, and then you're gone."

"Yeah, but that's me. And it's not easy."

Diesel disconnected, and I went back to my lunch. Macaroni and cheese, potato salad, turkey with gravy, macaroni and cheese, a dinner roll, three-bean salad, and more macaroni and cheese. I like macaroni and cheese.

A half hour later, Grandma was back at her video poker machine, and Briggs and I were standing guard. I was hoping Diesel would have a plan when he arrived, because I had no idea what to do with Grandma. It's not like I could put her in handcuffs and drag her home.

I caught a flash of fire-engine red in my peripheral vision and realized it was Lula's hair making its way across the casino floor.

"You're not gonna believe this," Lula said, coming up to me. "I was rolling crap at the craps table . . ."

"Easy come, easy go," Briggs said. "So much for the lucky money theory."

"Yeah, but turns out it **was** lucky. The guy standing next to me was some big-ass photographer on a photo shoot for some lingerie company, and he said they were looking for experienced plus-size models. He gave me his card, and he said I should just show up tomorrow first thing in the morning. I almost peed my pants right there. This here's my opportunity. I always wanted to be a supermodel. And a super-model's just one step away from being a celebrity."

"Just what the world needs," Briggs said. "One more big fat celebrity."

Lula narrowed her eyes at him. "Did you just say I was fat? Is that what I just heard? Because my ears better be wrong, or I'll grind you into midget dust."

"**Little** person," Briggs said. "I'm a **little person**."

"Hunh," Lula said. "If it was me, I'd rather be a midget. It's got a good sound to it. 'Little person' sounds like you should be in kindergarten."

Briggs was hands on hips, leaning forward. "How'd you like a punch in the nose?"

Lula looked down at him. "How'd you like my thumb in your eye?"

"I didn't know you had experience modeling lingerie," Grandma said to Lula.

"Not modeling, exactly. I got more general experience. When I was a 'ho, I was famous for accessorizing with lingerie. Everybody knew if you wanted a 'ho in nice undies, you go to Lula's corner. And another thing, I'm always reading them fashion magazines. I know how to stand. And I got a beautiful smile."

Lula smiled for us.

Grandma squinted at Lula. "Look at that. You got a gold tooth in the front. It's all sparkly under the lights. I never noticed before."

"I got it last week," Lula said. "It's got a diamond chip in it. That's what makes it sparkle."

"So if the modeling doesn't work out, you could be a pirate," Briggs said.

"It's for when I sing with Sally Sweet and his band," Lula said. "We changed our focus to rap. Sally's breakin' new ground. He's like the premier drag rapper."

Sally Sweet drives a school bus in Trenton during the day and does bar gigs on weekends. He looks like Howard Stern, and he dresses like Madonna. I had a mental picture of Sally rapping in drag, and it wasn't pretty.

"How are you doing at the video poker?" Lula asked Grandma.

"I'm not doing so good," Grandma said. "Maybe I just got to get warmed up."

"That's the way it works," Lula said. "First you got bad luck, and then you got the good luck."

My cell phone buzzed in my pocket. It was my mother.

"Where are you?" she asked.

"I'm at Daffy's in Atlantic City."

"Did you find your grandmother?"

"Yes. She's playing the slots."

"Do **not** leave her side. And do **not** put her on the bus to come home. God knows where she could end up."

"Right," I said to my mother. "No bus."

"Call me when you get on the road so I know when to expect you and your grandmother."

"Sure."

I disconnected and looked at Grandma hunched on her seat, back to punching the PLAY button, and wondered if it was a felony if you kidnapped your own grandmother. I suspected it would be the only way I'd get her to go home.

"I'm going shopping," Lula said. "I gotta look good tomorrow morning for my supermodel debut. And I know this is plus-size lingerie, but maybe I should go to the gym and try to lose ten or fifteen pounds. I bet I could do it if I put my mind to it."

I looked past Lula and locked eyes with the little man in the green pants. He was openly staring, watching us from the other side of the casino floor. I crooked my finger at him in a **come here** gesture, and he sidestepped behind a row of slots and disappeared. I took off across the room, but couldn't find him.

Lula was gone when I got back. Briggs was asleep on top of the duffel bag. And Grandma was staring at the poker machine.

"I'm not feeling so good," Grandma said. "My button finger is all swollen, and I'm sort of dizzy. I can't take the lights flashing at me anymore."

"We should go home."

"I can't go home. I gotta stay here and wait for my luck to get good. I got myself one of them high roller rooms this morning. I'm gonna take a nap."

I toed Briggs, and he jumped off the bag, eyes wide open, ready to be the wolverine.

"What?" he asked.

"Grandma wants to go to her room."

Ten minutes later, I had Grandma locked in her room with the money and Briggs standing guard outside her door.

"I'm going to check on Connie," I told Briggs. "Call me on my cell when Grandma gets up."

I walked down the hall, took the elevator to the casino floor, and found Connie still at the blackjack table. She had fifteen dollars in chips in front of her.

"This is **not** lucky money," Connie said. "I haven't won once . . . and I broke a nail."

The guy sitting next to her looked like he bludgeoned people for a living. Not that this would bother Connie, since half her family looked like this . . . and some for good reason.

"It was real ugly when she broke the nail," the guy said. "She used words I haven't heard since I was in the army." He leaned close to Connie. "If you want to get lucky, I could help you out."

"I don't need to get lucky that bad," Connie said.

"Just offering. No need to get mean," he said.

I wandered the casino looking for the little man in the green pants. I patrolled the gambling floor, browsed through a couple shops, checked out the bar and the café. No little man in green pants. Truth is, I was relieved. I mean, what the heck would I do with him if I found him? I had no legal right to apprehend him. And it seemed to me Grandma had sort of stolen his money. What would I say if he demanded it back?

I found a machine that I liked, took a seat, and slid a dollar into the money-sucker slot. Forty-five seconds later, my dollar was history and the machine went silent. I felt no compulsion to insert a second dollar. I love the casinos, but gambling isn't my passion. I like the neon and the noise and the optimism. I love that people come here with unrealistic hope. The energy is palpable. Okay, so sometimes it's fueled by greed and sloth and addiction. And sometimes the energy dissipates into despair. The way I see it, it's a little like driving the turnpike through Newark. The turnpike will get you to your destination faster, but there's always the possibility that you'll crash and die. It's the Jersey way, right? Take a chance. Act like a moron.

I felt all the little hairs stand up at the back of my neck and suspected Diesel had invaded my air space. I swiveled in my seat and found him standing behind me.

"How's it going?" he asked.

"I lost."

"I can fix that."

He fed a dollar into the machine and

bells dinged and bonged, lights flashed, and the machine paid out four hundred and twenty dollars.

I rolled my eyes at him, and he grinned down at me.

"This is nothing," he said. "You should see me shoot craps."

"I saw your little man in the green pants."

"Here?"

"Yep. I ran after him, but he disappeared."

"What was he doing?" Diesel asked.

"Watching Grandma."

Two older women in velour running suits paused on their way through the slots to appreciate Diesel. They looked him up and down and smiled.

"Ladies," Diesel said, returning their smiles.

One of the women winked at him, and they moved on.

Diesel mashed the PAYOUT button and

the machine printed a chit for the money. He tucked the chit into my sweatshirt pocket and pulled me off the stool. "Let's go on a Snuggy hunt."

"Why is he called Snuggy?"

"He gets into snug places . . . like bank vaults. Where's Grandma?"

"Taking a nap in her room. Briggs is in front of her door standing guard."

Diesel was holding my hand, walking us through the casino, and I could feel heat radiating up my arm. When the heat hit my shoulder and started to head south, I was going to disengage.

Daffy barked two o'clock and laser beams shot out of his eyes and danced across the casino ceiling. The old folks were lethargic after stuffing themselves at the lunch buffet and barely noticed. The dog barked "Yankee Doodle," and casino-wide, people self-medicated for acid reflux and irritable bowel. The day was already winding down. The senior buses would begin loading at four, and by five, the casino would be a graveyard. At six, the night-timers would start arriving. They'd drink more and spend more and wear tighter clothes. The men would have more hair and the women would have bigger boobs. Or at least the boobs would sit higher.

"How do you expect to catch Snuggy?" I asked Diesel.

"I thought I'd drag you around the casino for an hour or two hoping to run into him. And if that doesn't work, I'll use Grandma as bait."

We meandered through the rows of slot machines and patrolled the gaming tables . . . roulette, craps, blackjack. We checked out the bar and the café and the shops. We left the hotel and stood on the Boardwalk. A low cloud cover had moved in and the wind had picked up. The ocean was gray and foamy in front of us. Some rollers and choppy waves. No one on the beach. There was some Boardwalk foot traffic, but heads were down and sweat-shirts were zipped.

Diesel looked like he belonged here. Sin City behind him and the wild, untamable sea in front of him. I had a hunch I looked like I belonged in Macy's shoe department.

"Now what?" I said to him.

"Call Briggs and see if Grandma's up and ready to play."

"She's sleeping," Briggs said, answering on the second ring. "I can hear her snor-ing. Probably half the hotel can hear her snoring. She sounds like she's trying to suck her face into her nose. It's giving me a headache. And I hafta go to the can. I need a break here."

Diesel and I went back into the hotel and rode the elevator to Grandma's floor. Randy Briggs took off, and Diesel and I sat on the carpeted floor with our backs to the wall.

"Tell me about Snuggy," I said to Diesel.

Diesel had one knee bent and one long leg stretched out in front of him. "Snuggy gives me a cramp in my ass. This is the second time I've had to chase him down. The first time, I found him in a goat tent halfway up Everest. And I am **not** an Everest kind of guy. Everest is cold. And when you get tired of looking at rock, you can look at more rock." Diesel closed his eyes. "I'm more a tropical breezes and palm trees swaying man."

"What about Trenton? Do you like Trenton?"

"Does it have palm trees?"

"No."

"There's your answer," Diesel said.

"Are you after Snuggy because he stole the money?"

"No. I was after him before that. He stole a horse and was recognized leaving the scene. I was asked to put him on ice until the mess could get cleaned up. Problem is, Snuggy's like smoke. Hard to hang on to."

"And he doesn't want to be put on ice?"

"He claims it'll interfere with his life's work."

"Which is?"

"Apparently, it's stealing shit," Diesel said.

"Not many people steal horses these days."

"Guess he likes horses. He used to be a jockey. He'd win the race by some odd stroke of fate and then fall off the horse after it crossed the finish line. That's his M.O. He's unbelievably lucky, but he bungles everything. Yesterday, he stole close to a million dollars from Lou Delvina, got caught on Delvina's security tape, and managed to leave the money sitting on the curb for your grandmother to find."

Lou Delvina was a local mobster and a very scary guy. Diesel and I had a run-in with him not too long ago, and I wasn't thrilled about the idea that I was indirectly involved with him again.

"So your target is lucky, rides horses, likes green pants, and isn't smart. Anything else?" I asked Diesel.

"He talks to animals. Two-way conversations," Diesel said.

"Like the horse whisperer and the pet psychic on television."

"Whatever."

"Can you talk to animals?" I asked him.

"Honey, I can barely talk to humans."

3

The elevator door opened toward the end of the hallway, and Snuggy stepped out. His eyes locked onto Diesel and me sitting on the floor and widened. "You!" Snuggy said.

Diesel got to his feet. "Surprise."

Snuggy turned and punched the DOWN button and clawed at the closed elevator doors.

"Cripes, that's so pathetic," Diesel said. "Stop clawing at the elevator and come over here."

"Faith and begorrah, I can't. My sainted mother is dying. I need to go to her bedside."

Diesel cut his eyes to me. "Add fake Irish accent and pathological liar to the list."

"That cuts to the quick," Snuggy said.

"I have a file on you," Diesel said. "Your birth name is Zigmond Kulakowski, you were born in Staten Island, and your mother died ten years ago."

"I **feel** Irish," Snuggy said. "I'm pretty sure I'm a leprechaun."

Diesel was hands on hips, looking like he'd heard this before. "It doesn't say leprechaun in your file. And here's some bad news—a closet full of green pants doesn't make you a leprechaun."

"I'm Unmentionably lucky."

"Yeah, and I'm Unmentionably randy, but that doesn't make me a goat."

I stood and moved next to Diesel. "I want to know about the money my grandmother found. The money that belonged to Lou Delvina."

Snuggy slumped a little. "I needed cash, and I heard Delvina had a safe filled with numbers money. I mean, if you have to steal something, steal something that's already dirty, right? I know Delvina works his operation out of a car wash on Hamilton and Beacon Street, so I went to the car wash just as it was getting ready to open for business. And here's the lucky part. Everyone, including Delvina, was around back, looking at a broken water valve. The door to the office was wide open. I went in, saw the duffel bag sitting all by itself on the front desk, looked inside, saw the money, and walked out with it. I set the bag on the car roof while I looked for my keys, and then I forgot about it and drove away. I guess the bag slid off when I turned the corner. I came back and saw the old lady dragging it down the street. I tell you, some people have no scruples. I was perfectly nice, explaining to her how I lost the bag, and she told me to kiss off. And then she called me some rude names!"

"She said you couldn't identify the amount of money in the bag."

"I hadn't counted it. I didn't know how much there was. I'd only just stole it. Faith and begorrah."

"You say 'faith and begorrah' again, and I'm going to hit you," Diesel said.

"You can't hit me," Snuggy said. "I'm old, and I'm half your size."

"Yeah, it'd be embarrassing," Diesel said, "but I think I could force myself to do it."

Snuggy shuffled foot to foot. "Well, anyway, the money's mine. And I want it back."

"I think it might be finders keepers, losers weepers," I told Snuggy. "And besides, Grandma's spent a lot of it."

Snuggy went bug-eyed and a red scald started to creep from his neck to the top of his head. "What? No way! I need that money. It's a matter of life or death. They'll kill Doug!"

Oh boy. "Who's Doug?"

"He's a horse. Douglas Iron Man III. We've known each other for years. He was a four-year-old when I retired. He was really something back then. He won the Preakness. Anyway, times have been hard for him lately. I ran into him last week when I went to visit a friend in Rumson. They had Doug in a stall, waiting to get put down. He had a sore on his leg, and they'd decided it'd be too costly to treat."

"That's so sad."

"It's more than sad. It's criminal. Poor Doug. He was really depressed. He could hardly pick his head up. He looked at me with those big brown eyes, and I knew I had to do something. So I returned that night, and I sneaked him out and drove him to Trenton. My cousin has a house on Mulberry Street, and he let me put Doug in his garage until I could make arrangements for his leg operation.

There's a real good equine veterinary hospital in Pennsylvania. Problem was, I had to get the money to pay for Doug's care. When I heard about Delvina, I thought it was perfect. It's not like he earned the money and deserved it. I figured it was better spent on Doug."

I nodded. "Makes perfect sense."

"It didn't make perfect sense to the guy who owned the horse," Diesel said. "He woke up missing a horse. And he wasn't happy."

"I left a note," Snuggy said. "I even offered to buy Doug."

"We have people working to smooth things over," Diesel said. "Until that happens, you and Doug need to keep a low profile. Doug can't stay in a garage in Trenton."

"It's worse than you think," Snuggy said. "Delvina followed me to the garage last night and took Doug. Now he's holding him for ransom. Delvina wants his money. All of it. Or else he'll do something terrible to Doug."

"Great," Diesel said. "It wasn't bad enough that I had to find a guy who thinks he's a leprechaun, now I have to rescue a horse."

"He's not just any old horse," Snuggy said. "He's very intelligent. And he's sensitive. It hurt his feelings when he found out they weren't going to fix his leg. He worked hard all those years to stay in shape so he could win races. And then he was put out to stud, and he worked night and day impregnating mares. And it's not like they were all love matches. Doug said sometimes they were downright cranky."

"Maybe Doug should have paid closer attention," I said. "**No** is **no**."

"It was his **job**," Snuggy said. "He was caught between a rock and a hard place."

Diesel gave a snort of laughter.

"You're supposed to help me," Snuggy said to Diesel.

"No," Diesel said. "I'm supposed to remove you from action so you don't do something stupid and end up on **Letterman** telling everyone you talk to animals."

"Jeez," I said. "I feel really bad about this. I can't just walk away and let Delvina kill Doug."

Diesel looked like he had another cramp in his ass. "You're not going all girly and gushy on me over this horse, are you?"

"I am absolutely **not** relegating some poor horse to the glue factory just because he has a sore on his leg. It's a horse! Horses are amazing."

"Have you ever seen one up close?" Diesel asked.

"Not lately. But they look wonderful on television. And I read all the Walter Farley books about the Black Stallion."

Diesel choked back a smile. He thought I was amusing. "Do you know where Delvina is keeping Doug?" he asked Snuggy.

"No."

"How do you get in touch with Delvina?"

"He calls me. He gave me until three o'clock tomorrow to return the money. He said if he didn't get it by three, he'd shoot Doug."

"That's plenty of time," I said. "We just get the money from Grandma and give it to Delvina. Probably he won't notice if there's a little missing. These things happen, right?"

I called Lula. "Don't spend any more of that money," I told her. "We need it."

"Too late," she said. "It's all gone. And I'm wearing everything I bought. I'm dressed in my supermodel clothes. And I was real lucky on account of I found that photographer at the craps table and he took pictures of me so I'd have a portfolio tomorrow morning."

"Uh-oh."

"What **uh-oh**? There's no **uh-oh**. It's all good. He spent a hour taking pictures, and he said they were the most fabulous he's ever done."

"Did you pay him to take the pictures?"

"Yeah. It was expensive, but it was worth the money. I tell you, he knows what he's doing."

"Where is he now?"

"I don't know. I just come back to the casino, and he didn't come with me. We took the pictures outside. It was cold, but he said the light was real good. Where are you?"

"I'm on the fourteenth floor. I'm waiting for Grandma to wake up. She wanted to take a nap."

"I'll come up there."

I disconnected and called Connie.

"Are you still at the blackjack table?"

"Yeah."

"I don't suppose you have any money left?"

"Nope. Lost every last cent."

"Maybe you'd better come up to the fourteenth floor. We have a situation."

Grandma's door opened, and Grandma stuck her head out. "What's going on?" She spotted Snuggy and sucked in some air. "It's the robber! I'd know him any-where." She ducked into her room and, an instant later, was in the hall with a gun in her hand. She squeezed off a shot and took out a wall sconce before Diesel could disarm her.

"She's insane!" Snuggy said. "She's a crazy woman. Someone do something."

"Must be something wrong with that gun," Grandma said. "I don't usually miss by that much."

"He's lucky," I told Grandma.

"I'm pretty sure I'm a leprechaun," Snuggy said.

Grandma eyeballed him. "I guess that could explain it."

Diesel emptied the gun, pocketed the shells, and gave the gun back to Grandma. "Do you have any idea how much money you've spent?"

"No. I wasn't paying attention. Randy was keeping track of that." She looked around. "Where is he?"

"He went to the men's room."

"Maybe the leprechaun made him disappear," Grandma said. "Everybody knows you can't trust a leprechaun."

I told Grandma about Doug and Lou Delvina.

"Sounds like a lot of baloney," Grandma said.

"I've got pictures," Snuggy said, taking his phone out of his pocket. "I took pictures so I could send them to the vet in Pennsylvania."

We all looked over Snuggy's shoulder at the pictures of Doug.

"He looks real, all right," Grandma said. "And he's a beauty. He's got pretty eyes."

Lula stepped out of the elevator and made her way over to us. "What are we looking at?"

I filled her in on Doug and Delvina, and I checked out her new clothes. Spike-heeled gold Louboutins, metallic gold miniskirt, and a long black satin tuxedo jacket. She took the jacket off and she was wearing a gold bustier that wasn't nearly big enough to contain **the girls**.

Snuggy was eyeball-to-headlight with Lula, and he looked like he'd swallowed his tongue when she turned to face him. Diesel was rocked back on his heels, smiling. I'm solidly heterosexual, but I have to admit, I was mesmerized by the sight of all that boob spilling out over the gold top.

"Boy, you got some hooters in that

getup," Grandma said to Lula. "I wouldn't mind having an outfit like that."

"I was worried it might not fit just right," Lula said.

"It looks good from down here," Snuggy said.

"I'm not complaining," Diesel told her.

The elevator **bing**ed and Connie stepped out. "What's going on?"

I repeated the Doug and Delvina story, and Connie got a look at the photo.

"We gotta rescue this horse," Lula said. "I can't take a chance on crappin' up my karma now that I'm gonna be a super-model."

"What's with all this feng shui and karma stuff?" Connie asked Lula.

"I got my horoscope done, and it said I needed to be more spiritual. I looked into being a Catholic and it sounded like a real pain in the ass, so I'm going with Asian shit."

"I guess I wouldn't mind giving my money over to save Doug," Grandma said. "And I still got my RV, so I'm pretty lucky when you think about it."

We all trooped into Grandma's room and waited while Diesel counted the money.

"We have six hundred and forty thousand," Diesel said to Snuggy. "How much did Delvina say you stole?"

"Eight hundred and ninety thousand."

Diesel dumped the money back into the bag and zipped it closed. "We're short a quarter of a million."

"I went through ten," Connie said.

"I went through another ten," Lula said.

"I got a good price on the RV," Grandma said. "It was only thirty thousand. And I paid some to Randy for guarding the money and driving the RV."

Diesel was smiling at Grandma. "You blew through almost two hundred thousand and you were playing dollar slots? That's impressive."

"Especially since some of that time I was winning," Grandma said.

"Twelve dollars?"

"Yep. I was on a roll."

"Delvina isn't going to be happy," Snuggy said. "He wanted **all** his money back."

"Delvina shouldn't get any of that money back," Diesel said. "Delvina's lucky he's still alive and walking upright."

"Yeah, but we gotta think about the horse," Lula said. "We gotta focus on the horse. How're we gonna get the horse safe and sound?"

"Why don't you do something lucky?" Grandma said to Snuggy. "You're the leprechaun. You're supposed to go around finding pots of gold."

"I could, except you need a rainbow to follow, and it was cloudy today. And I can't do it at night. And anyway, I'm a Polish/Irish leprechaun, so the pot of gold business might not work for me. Mostly, I find it's easier to steal the gold."

"I got a idea," Lula said. "Suppose we take the money we have left, and we let it ride on the craps table. Okay, so we got a half-assed leprechaun, but this is still lucky money, right? I got lucky with it. And Grandma got lucky with it."

I looked over at Diesel. I knew who had the ability to win at craps. I suspected Diesel could make the spots change on the dice if he put his mind to it.

"No," Diesel said.

"I didn't say anything."

"You didn't have to. I know what you were thinking."

"Now you're reading minds?"

"Cutie Pie, that thought flashed in neon across your forehead."

"I don't think it's a good idea to gamble

with **all** the money," Snuggy said. "Maybe we should each take a small amount and see how it goes."

"It's your money and your horse," Diesel said. "How much do you want to hand out?"

"A thousand apiece," Snuggy said.

Diesel gave Lula, Connie, Grandma, and Snuggy a thousand and didn't take any for himself.

"Where's Randy?" Grandma asked. "I need him to guard my money while I get lucky."

I called Briggs on my cell phone.

"Yeah," Briggs said.

"Where are you?"

"I'm with a girl. She's twice my size and half my age and I'm busy. What do you want?"

"Grandma's awake and wants to go back to the casino."

"Jeez, give her a pill or something. I think I'm in love here."

"How long do you think this love will last?"

"Ten minutes. Twenty, tops."

I disconnected Briggs.

"Briggs is temporarily indisposed," I told Grandma. "I'll hold the bag for you."

"Okay, let's do it," Grandma said. "Let's kick some behind in this casino."

"What about you?" I asked Diesel.

"I'm babysitting the leprechaun."

"Was that sarcasm?" Snuggy asked.

Diesel held the door for him. "You have a problem with sarcasm?"

4

We all piled into the elevator and took it to the casino level. Snuggy and Diesel walked off toward the blackjack tables. Lula headed for roulette. And Connie and I followed Grandma to her favorite video poker machine.

"I can feel a big payday coming up," Grandma said. "I was just getting warmed up before."

We got Grandma settled in, and Connie nudged me.

"Look across the aisle at the blackjack table closest to us," Connie said. "I think that's Billy Major in the striped shirt."

Billy Major has a stable of hookers who

work the projects. To my knowledge, he's never been arrested for procuring. However, he has been arrested several times for possession of controlled substances, and the latest charge was outstanding. Billy Major was on my list of active skips. Major failed to appear for his court appearance, and until this moment, I hadn't been able to locate him. Probably because I was looking in Trenton, and he obviously was in Atlantic City.

I had a credit card and twenty dollars in my back pocket. My purse with all my bounty hunter paraphernalia was upstairs in Grandma's room. "I haven't got any equipment on me," I said to Connie.

Connie's purse was on her shoulder. She rooted around in it and came up with cuffs and a stun gun and a semi-automatic Smith & Wesson .45. I took the cuffs and stun gun and left her with the Smith & Wesson. Connie was a lot tougher than I was, but capturing felons was on my side of the division of labor.

I wedged the duffel bag with the remaining money between Grandma's stool and the poker machine. "I'll be right back," I told her. "In the meantime, keep your eye on the money."

I crossed the aisle and stood behind Major for a couple minutes, watching him play. I had the cuffs tucked into the back pocket of my jeans and the stun gun in my sweatshirt pocket. The dealer shuffled the cards, and I leaned over Major.

"Excuse me," I said, close to his ear. "Billy Major?"

"Yeah."

He turned and looked at me, and recognition registered. This wasn't the first time I'd apprehended him.

"Oh shit," Major said.

I clapped a cuff on him, and he yelped and jumped, knocking into the gaming table, sending chips flying. Everyone stood, the dealer called for security, overturned drinks dripped onto the carpet.

I struggled to get the second cuff on Major. "Bond enforcement. Hold still!"

"Fuck this," Major said, ripping the cuffs out of my hands, taking off for the exit on the far side of the room.

He had a head start, but he was hampered by high-heeled boots and forty pounds of gold chains hanging around his neck. He was plowing into people, but I was trying to be careful, dodging cocktail waitresses and casino guests. He crashed into an old woman with a walker and stumbled, and I took a flying leap and tackled him. My momentum took us to the ground.

I've never had formal martial arts training. Mostly, I rely on the fact that men tend to underestimate my desperation. I curled my fingers into Major's shirt, knowing casino security would help secure him if I could just hang on until they arrived. We were tumbling around, and I caught a flash of gold in my peripheral vision and realized it was Lula.

"Outta my way," Lula said.

I rolled off, and Lula sat down hard on Major. Major let out a **woof** of air, farted, and went inert.

An old man looked down at Major. "He's dead."

Lula got off Major, I attached the second cuff, and Major still didn't move. We all took a closer look.

"I might have seen him breathe just then," Lula said.

"I got a defibrillator on my Rascal," someone said. "You want to try to jump-start him?"

"I got oxygen," someone else said.

Lula got her foot under Major and

turned him over. His eyes were open. His lips were pressed tight together.

"Christ," Major said through clenched teeth.

"He just got breathless," Lula said. "I have that effect on men on account of I'm a supermodel."

The security guys had arrived and were mixed in with the gawkers. The gawkers looked like they were enjoying themselves, but security didn't look happy.

Connie pushed her way through the crowd, corralled the senior rent-a-cop, showed him her documentation, and vouched for me as her representative. The gawkers began to disperse, and two tables down, I could see Diesel smiling at me. I flipped him the bird, and the smile widened.

"What are we gonna do with this fool?" Lula wanted to know. "I'd take him back, but I got my photo shoot tomorrow morning. I'm sleeping here so I wake up fresh as a daisy. Grandma said I could bunk with her. She's got that big ol' suite with a pull-out couch."

"I'll take him," Connie said. "I haven't got my gambling mojo going today. Let me borrow your Firebird, and I'll give you my thousand."

"Deal," Lula said. "I'm feeling hot. I probably don't need the extra thousand, but I'll take it just in case."

We dragged Major to his feet and walked him out of the casino into the parking garage. We got shackles out of the trunk of Lula's car, trussed Major up, and put him into the backseat. Connie got behind the wheel, and we watched her drive away.

"That was lucky," Lula said. "We caught a scumbag. And we didn't even kill him."

The casino was relatively empty when we returned to the gaming floor. The day-players were settling themselves into their buses. The night-timers were sitting in traffic on the Parkway. Attendants quietly swept carpets and collected empty glasses. The big Daffy Dog was silent.

"I'm going to the café for a burger," Lula said. "How about you?"

"I need to get back to Grandma. I left her alone with the money."

I hustled back to the gaming floor, and I saw Briggs before I saw Grandma. He was standing behind her, as always, but he wasn't guarding the duffel bag. Grandma was playing the poker machine, and Briggs was back on his heels, looking bored. And the duffel bag was missing.

"Where's the money?" I asked him.

"I put it in the hotel vault," Briggs said.

"It's not like I could spend it," Grandma said, punching the PLAY button. "I figured I might as well put it away where it was safe. Then Randy don't have to carry that big heavy bag around. We're almost done here anyway. It's amazing how fast you can go through a thousand dollars when you got the knack for it."

"Have you won anything?"

"Not a darn nickel. It's just as good, though, on account of I want to get back to the room to watch some television. Starting at seven o'clock, there's reruns of **Dancing with the Stars**."

I left Grandma and Briggs and walked over to Snuggy and Diesel. Snuggy was playing blackjack, and Diesel was standing behind him.

"How's it going?" I asked Diesel.

"I don't think it looks good for the horse."

"Snuggy hasn't got a lot of chips in front of him."

"He consistently gets great cards, but he's the worst blackjack player ever."

"Why don't you want to play?" I asked Diesel.

"Can't. I've won here too many times. If I sit down, I'll be asked to leave."

"They can do that?"

"They think I cheat," Diesel said.

"Do you?"

"Yeah." Diesel smiled down at me. "I liked the tag team wrestling exhibition."

"You could have helped!"

"You were doing okay without me. Who was the guy you took down?"

"Billy Major. He's a Trenton pimp who got caught in a drug sting. Vinnie bonded him out, and then Major failed to appear for a court appearance. It was dumb luck that Connie spotted him."

Snuggy was fidgeting in his seat and cracking his knuckles. Nervous. Knowing he was screwing up. He had only a few chips left.

"This is painful," I said to Diesel. "He should be playing something that's pure chance."

"There are decisions to be made with all the games," Diesel said. "Even with slots. And he's incapable of making a good decision."

Lula huffed up to us, clearly on a rant, hands waving in the air. "This place is fixed," Lula said. "I guess I know when I'm hot. And I was hot. And I lost. How could that be? I got a mind to report this to someone." She looked over at Snuggy. "Don't look like he's doing too good, either. I tell you, this place is rigged. Where's Grandma?"

"She went back to her room to watch a **Dancing with the Stars** retrospective."

"No kidding? I love that show. Maybe I should go watch with her. I think I got high blood pressure from losing all that money. I got a headache. What kind of headache do you get from high blood pressure? Is it on the top of your head? Is it behind your left eyeball? Does it go down the back of your neck? I got all of those. Maybe I'm having a stroke. Is anything sagging on me?"

"Not that I can see," I told her. Thanks to the miracle of spandex.

Lula left, and I cut my eyes to Diesel.

"Don't give me that look," Diesel said. "She asked about sagging, and I didn't say anything."

"You were thinking."

"Now you're a mind reader?"

"It was flashing in neon across your forehead."

Diesel grabbed me and hugged me to him. "Cute."

The night crowd was beginning to filter into the casino. Young singles coming directly from work. Older couples in that awkward age, caught between assisted living and the family home in suburbia. Hard-core addicted gamblers who had spent all day sleeping off a hangover and were now ready to repeat the last night's disaster. The noise level rose and dealers notched up the action.

"That's it," Snuggy said, pushing back from the table. "I'm done. I lost all my money. I feel terrible."

A cocktail waitress sidled up to Diesel. "Can I get you something? **Anything?**"

"No," Diesel said, "but thanks for asking."

I did an eye roll, and the waitress sashayed away.

"How are we going to get the money for Doug?" Snuggy asked. "We only have until three o'clock tomorrow."

"I know we all like Doug," Diesel said. "But maybe it's his time."

Snuggy looked horrified, and I smacked Diesel on the back of his head.

"He's a horse," Diesel said. "Do you know how many horses you could buy for a quarter of a million? Lots. And they could be under the hood of a car."

"There are a bunch of casinos here," I

said. "Surely one of them would let you play."

"Sorry, sugar. I'm persona non grata. These casinos put me through M.I.T."

I was speechless. "You graduated from M.I.T.?" I finally managed.

"Just because I'm big doesn't mean I'm stupid."

"You look like a street person."

"I like to be comfortable. Anyway, lots of women think I'm sexy like this." He smiled and ruffled my hair. "Not you, maybe, but lots of other women."

I did another eye roll.

"You keep doing that and you're gonna shake something loose in there," Diesel said.

"So you haven't always chased after bad guys?"

"I started doing this in my teens. Mostly part-time."

"Like Buffy the Vampire Slayer?"

"Yeah, except I don't mess with vampires. And I think Buffy might not be real."

"And you're real?"

"As real as a guy could get."

"Okay, great. Now we've established we're all real," Snuggy said. "Could we get back to the Doug problem?"

"I need an off-site poker game," Diesel said. "Private. High-stakes party."

Snuggy pumped his fist into the air. "Yes! I knew you'd come through. You guys stay here and I'll find a game. I'll ask around."

"You aren't going to take off on me, are you?" Diesel asked Snuggy. "Because I'd track you down and find you and the rest wouldn't be pretty."

"You got my word."

"Your word isn't worth squat," Diesel said. "Just remember my promise. Make sure no one in the game knows me. And find out if they're checking guns at the door."

"Okay, got that," Snuggy said. "Why do you want to know about the guns? Are you packing?"

"No. I don't want to get shot when I win. It hurts. We're going to the café. You can catch me there or you can call Stephanie on her cell."

Snuggy wandered away and Diesel stuck his hand into my sweatshirt pocket.

"Hey!" I said.

"I'm looking for your voucher."

"I bet."

"I need the receipt I gave you when I cashed out the slot."

"I put it in my jeans pocket. I didn't want to lose it."

"Even better."

I stepped back from him. "I can get it!"

"You're not a whole lot of fun," Diesel said.

"I have a boyfriend."

"And?"

I pulled the receipt out of my pocket

and gave it to Diesel. "And I don't mess around."

"Admirable but boring." Diesel took the receipt and towed me across the room to the cashier. "It wouldn't kill you to flirt a little, so I don't remember this assignment as totally sucking. I'm babysitting a guy who thinks he's a leprechaun, and I'm rescuing a has-been horse. The least you could do is grab my ass once in a while."

"Suppose I just **think** about grabbing your ass?"

"Better than nothing."

Diesel gave his receipt to the cashier and collected his winnings. "This is burger money," Diesel said, draping an arm across my shoulders, moving me toward the café.

5

We were finishing burgers and fries when Snuggy rolled into the café.

"I got you into a game," Snuggy said. "It's at Caesars, but it's not got anything to do with the hotel. Strictly private party. Lots of money involved. Starts at ten." He gave Diesel a slip of paper. "Here's the room number, and the guy's name. You ask for him, and they'll let you in. You gotta have ten thousand to start."

I looked over at Diesel. "Do you have ten thousand?"

"Not yet."

"How are you going to get it?"

"I'll take it out of the money in the duffel bag."

Snuggy looked over his shoulder, back at the entrance to the café.

"Is there a problem?" Diesel asked.

Snuggy dragged his attention back to us. "No. Everything's good."

A half hour later, we were knocking on Grandma's door.

"You're just in time," Lula said, letting us in, trotting back to the couch and wedging herself in between Grandma and Briggs. "This here's the beginning of that show where they made what's-her-name cry 'cause she wasn't hot enough. And then after that one is the time the fat chick wore the ugly blue dress."

Diesel had his mouth to my ear. "She's kidding, right?"

"Don't you watch television?"

"Yeah. Ball games, boxing, hockey."

"This isn't any of those," I told him.

Grandma had a two-room suite. The bedroom had a king-size bed, bureau, and two boudoir chairs. The sitting room had a large couch, a desk and chair, a comfy club chair and ottoman. The walls were butter yellow, dotted with pictures of beagles. The carpet was yellow with black dog paw prints. The draperies, couch, and chairs were done up in a yellow, orange, and white floral-print fabric. It was like the Snoopy Room at the insane asylum.

"What do you think of the room?" Grandma asked. "Don't you think it's cheery?"

"Yep," I said. "Very cheery."

Diesel was back at my ear. "If I stay in here too long, I'll have a seizure."

"We came to get some money from the bag," I said. "Diesel needs it."

"You have to wait," Briggs said. "I don't want to miss this part. The money's all the way down in the vault. You have to go to the desk, and they take you down two flights, where they've got safety deposit boxes for hotel guests. It's a whole big deal. It'll take a half hour, and I'll miss the rest of the show."

"Can I get the money?" Diesel asked.

"No. I put the money in, and I'm the only one who can get the money out. You need a picture ID, and they do a fingerprint scan. It's like Fort Knox."

"What kind of show is this?" Diesel asked. "They're dancing."

"**Dancing with the Stars**," I told him. "Dancing **with the Stars**."

"I'd jump off a cliff if I had to watch this every week."

"Suppose you got to eat birthday cake while you watched it?"

"That would help," Diesel said, "but it wouldn't close the deal."

"This is over at nine o'clock," Briggs said. "Can you wait until then?"

"I guess," Diesel said.

"I'm staying here," Snuggy said. "I like this show."

I pushed in next to Grandma. "Me, too."

"Do these dancers ever hit each other?" Diesel asked.

"No."

"Then I'm gonna pass. I'll be back at nine."

It was nine o'clock and Briggs was ready to go. Grandma was asleep in her bedroom. Lula and Snuggy were watching SPEED channel.

Diesel knocked once and opened the door.

"Why do you knock here, but you just pop into my apartment unannounced?" I asked him.

"I don't want to chance seeing some of these people naked. You're not one of them."

"Let's move," Briggs said. "I got a date tonight. I don't want to be late."

Diesel draped an arm across my shoulders. "I have a plan."

That was good since I didn't have any plans of my own. I was tired of watching television and tired of hanging out in the casino. I didn't have a room. I didn't have a way to get home. I didn't have any money. I'd called Morelli to tell him I didn't know when I'd be back in Trenton, and I'd gotten his phone service. That meant either he was called out on a case or the Rangers were playing and the game was televised.

"You're going to make me look civilized," Diesel said.

"How much time do I have?"

"Not enough. I just want you to come with me. I checked out the players and they're all older, and I doubt anyone's going to be wearing torn jeans. If I go by myself, I'll look like a hustler. If you come along, we can role-play." He turned to

Snuggy. "You are **not** to leave the room. If you leave the room, I'll send Lula out to get you. And you saw what she did to that guy in the casino."

Snuggy gasped and gave an involuntary shiver.

"Yep," Lula said to Snuggy. "I'd squash you like a bug if I had to."

Diesel, Briggs, and I took the elevator and walked across the casino floor to the front desk. Briggs flashed his ID and asked to see his safety deposit box. He was ushered into a back room, and the door closed behind him.

My cell phone buzzed in my pocket. I hauled it out and looked at the number display. Blocked. Most likely Morelli or Ranger.

"Yep?" I said into the phone.

"Your car's at the bonds office, and the electronics in your purse tell me you're in Atlantic City. Are you okay?"

It was Ranger. Ranger's former Special Forces, now turned security expert. Our history together isn't all that long, and it's hard to say how our future relationship will go. Ranger's personality and skin tone run several shades darker than Morelli's. He's a little bigger, got a little more bulk to his muscle. His hair is brown and currently cut short, and his eyes are black. And with or without clothes, he's a heart-stopper.

In the past, I've gotten myself into some precarious situations, and Ranger now feels compelled to monitor me. Since I have no control over Ranger, and because sometimes I actually like having him watch over me, I go with it.

"I'm here with Grandma, and Lula, and Randy Briggs, and a guy who thinks he's a leprechaun . . . and Diesel."

"Babe," Ranger said.

"And I'm fine."

"Stay that way," Ranger said. And he disconnected.

Diesel had his thumbs hooked into his pockets. "I'm guessing that wasn't your mother."

"It was Ranger."

"Doing a bed check?"

"He likes to know his family is safe."

"And the boyfriend, Morelli?"

"I called him earlier."

I've known Joe Morelli all my life. I know his family, his friends, his history. I know his sexual tastes, his favorite sports teams, his shoe size, his pizza preferences, his iPod playlist.

I've had to judge Ranger and Diesel on actions and attitude, and touch. Ranger's touch is firm. He feels comfortable assuming authority. Diesel's touch is surprisingly gentle. I think Diesel is afraid he'll leave a bruise.

"Can you make a quarter of a million on this game?" I asked him.

Diesel shrugged. "Hard to predict how a game will go. I'd have preferred something with higher stakes, but this is what Snuggy found for me so I'll do the best I can."

The door behind the registration desk opened, and Briggs walked out with an envelope in his hand. He gave the envelope to Diesel and answered his cell phone.

"I'm on my way," Briggs said into his phone. He listened to something said on the other end, and he giggled. "Gotta go," he told us. "Don't wait up."

Caesars Hotel and Casino was a couple blocks north. The Boardwalk was lit, but beyond it was black ocean and sky. The surf surged onto the beach and whooshed away, sight unseen, and mist swirled around overhead lights. I found an elastic scrunchie in my bag and tied my hair back into a ponytail before it frizzed out of control.

"The game is in a high roller suite," Diesel said. "The suite was occupied this afternoon, so I wasn't able to get in, but it probably has a living room area where you can hang out. Stay away from the poker table and stay awake. I'll be John Diesel, so remember to call me John."

"I thought you were just Diesel?"

"Not everyone is comfortable playing cards with a guy who has only one name."

The casino and shopping pier were in front of us. Professionally illuminated palaces of hope and recreation. Diesel steered me toward the shopping pier.

"We need to glam you up a little," he said. "The jeans are okay. The sweatshirt and sweater have to go."

"How about you? Are we going to glam you up?"

"No. I'm the hedge fund guy who's so rich he can wear whatever the hell he wants."

"And I'm . . ."

"You're the bimbo."

Fortunately, since I was born and raised in Trenton, I'm good at selecting bimbo clothes. I found a little white T-shirt that had SWEET THING written in sparkly pink glitter across the boobs. It was a size too small and was cut low on the top and sat an inch above my jeans to show maximum skin. I covered it with a black leather jacket that coordinated with my black-and-white Converse sneakers. I added some extra eyeliner and mascara, and I was ready to rock and roll.

Diesel smiled when I walked out of the dressing room. "If I didn't have to save a horse, I'd marry you."

"I'm not surprised. I always had you pegged for the bimbo type."

"Saves time," Diesel said.

We left the shops and crossed the Boardwalk to the casino. The gaming floor was similar to Daffy's. Substitute statue of Caesar for Big Brass Dog. Even on a weekday in March, it was packed. Colored neon pulsed around the room. Slot machines clanged and dinged. We went directly to the bank of elevators.

Minutes later, we were in the suite. The guy who answered the door was young. Early twenties. And big. Over six feet and bulked up with steroids. A rental goon hired to serve as doorman. The suite was luxurious, with an ocean view. Not much to see but black glass at this hour, but in the morning, it had to be spectacular. Five men were already seated around the poker table. They were all in their fifties. All overweight from booze and excess. They looked like carnivores. They studied us with mild curiosity.

Diesel nodded to them. "John Diesel."

"Diesel, like an engine. Are you a train engine or a truck engine?" one of the guys asked.

Diesel just smiled. Diesel heard that a lot.

"I'm Rocky," the guy said. "Who's the lady?"

"Stephanie," Diesel said.

"Hedging your bets in case you drop out early?"

"Brought her along for luck," Diesel said.

He gave me a light kiss on the top of my head and took his seat at the table. I got a soda from the bar and got comfy on the sofa. It was a big overstuffed affair with lots of throw pillows. Fresh flowers on the glass-topped coffee table. A plate of fresh fruit. There was a full buffet set out on the sideboard.

An hour later, I was still perched on the couch, watching the game. It had taken on a rhythm. Cards were dealt. Chips were moved. Not much was said. Diesel was looking pleasant, playing under the radar, staying in the game but not making a splash. I'd thought he'd be playing a role by now. Maybe drinking a lot or looking nervous. Instead, he'd chosen to almost disappear. It was a no-smoking room, but three of the men were smoking. One was smoking a cigar. No one objected. Diesel had a rum and Coke in front of him, but he'd only sipped at it.

Two of the six players had dropped out by midnight. Diesel and Rocky looked about even. The man to Diesel's left was sweating. His name was Walter, and he'd lost beyond his comfort zone. He laid his cards down and was done. He stood and left. Didn't look at me.

From my distance, it was hard to tell how much money was involved. Diesel and Rocky were the only players still working from their original stake. All others had added. Some had added a lot.

Diesel looked around at me. "Are you doin' okay, sugar?"

"Yeah," I said. "I'm fine. Are you done soon?"

"Hard to say."

"Maybe we want to up the ante now that we've separated the men from the boys," Rocky said to Diesel. And he pushed his chips into the middle of the table.

The guy opposite Diesel scraped back in his chair and stood. "Too rich for me. I'm out."

Diesel counted his chips. Not enough. "This is too bad because I have a real good hand, but I'm short. I tell you what. I'll throw Stephanie into the pot and call you."

I jumped off the couch. "What?"

Rocky looked over at me. "I guess she's cute enough. What's the deal?"

Diesel leaned back in his chair. "What do you want? The night? Twenty-four hours?"

"The night. I'm flying out in the morning."

"Hey, wait a minute," I said. "You can't bet me in a poker game."

"I'll buy you a new car tomorrow," Diesel said.

"What kind?"

"What kind do you want?"

"I want a Ferrari," I told him.

"Forget it. I'll buy you a Camry."

"Lexus."

"A **used** Lexus."

"No way," I told him.

Diesel took another look at his hand and at the money on the table. "Okay, I'll get you a new Lexus."

I bit into my lower lip. I was pretty sure Diesel knew what he was doing. I mean, he cheats, right?

"How good is your hand?" I asked him.

Diesel shrugged.

"She's kind of a pain in the ass," Rocky said.

Diesel rocked back in his chair and studied me. "She grows on you. Anyway, she's the best I've got to offer right now unless you want to take a check."

"What the hell," Rocky said. "What have you got?"

Diesel laid his cards on the table. "Straight flush. Jack high."

"Beats me. Four of a kind. All kings." He gave me the once-over for the second time. "Just as well. She'd probably give me a heart attack. She looks like a lot of work."

I narrowed my eyes at him. "Excuse me?"

"Don't get your panties in a bunch. I'm just saying."

I had my purse hung on my shoulder and my shopping bag in hand. I was ready to go. It was past my bedtime, and I was pissed off that everyone thought I wasn't such a great prize. All right, so I'm no Julia Roberts, but I had a nice nose, and I'd tweezed my eyebrows two days ago.

Diesel pocketed his winnings and moved to the door. "We should do this again sometime."

"I'm pretty sure you were cheating," Rocky said, "but I don't know how."

"I was lucky," Diesel said.

The rent-a-goon let us out and watched us walk to the elevator. We stepped in, and Diesel hit buttons for the fourth floor and the lobby. We got off at the fourth floor and took the stairs.

"Just in case," Diesel said. "Walter looked like he was going to shoot himself, but he might have changed his mind and decided it would be more satisfying to shoot me."

"How much did you win?"

"A hundred and ten thousand."

"That's a lot of money, but not enough."

"Delvina doesn't want to kill the horse. He wants his money, and I'm hoping he's smart enough to understand that half of something is better than all of nothing."

When we got to the second floor, Diesel took the service elevator to the ground level, and we exited through the kitchen. The staff didn't seem all that surprised. Probably people sneaked out like this all the time.

"Now what?" I asked Diesel.

"Now we go back to Daffy's and get a room."

"Two rooms."

I couldn't believe what I was hearing. "What do you mean there are no rooms?"

"There are four major conventions in town," the desk clerk said. "I've been calling around all night, trying to find rooms. If you want a room, you'll have to go off the Boardwalk."

It was almost one o'clock. Going off the Boardwalk at this hour in Atlantic City didn't sound like a good idea.

"We can drive back to Trenton and be home by two-thirty," I told Diesel.

Diesel had his hand at my back, moving me away from the desk. "Do you have a car?"

"No. We came in Lula's car, and Connie borrowed it to take the FTA back. Don't you have a car? How did you get here?"

"You don't really want to know the answer to that question, do you?"

"Do you think we could rent a car?"

"Not at this hour, but I could **borrow** a car," Diesel said.

"You mean **steal** a car?"

"Stealing implies permanence."

"Grandma has a suite. We can crash there for the night and find a way to get back to Trenton in the morning."

We took the elevator to the fourteenth floor, stepped out into the hall, and saw Lula sprawled on the carpet in front of Grandma's suite. She was changed out of the fancy gold outfit, and she was wide awake, flat on her back with a pillow under her head.

"And?" I said to her.

"And I can't sleep, is what. I got my big photo shoot first thing in the morning. I need my beauty rest, and I can't sleep with your grandma snoring. I've never heard anything like it. It's not normal snoring. I tried to get my own room, but there's no rooms left."

"Where's Snuggy?" Diesel asked.

"He's still in there."

The door to the suite opened, and Snuggy lurched out. "I can't take it anymore. I need sleep."

Lula was on her feet. "Me, too. What are we gonna do?"

"Let's kill her," Snuggy said.

"Works for me," Lula said. "How you want to do it? Smother her with a pillow?"

The elevator **bing**ed, and Briggs hopped out. "What's everyone doing in the hall? And what's that disgusting sound? It sounds like King Kong with a sinus infection."

"It's Grandma snoring," I told him.

"We haven't got any place to sleep. The hotel is full, and no one can sleep with Grandma. Where do you sleep?"

"I sleep in the RV. I just came back to make sure everything was okay here."

Lula's eyes opened wide. "I bet the RV has lots of room. It probably can sleep lots of people."

"Five," Briggs said.

"We're five," Lula said. "Imagine that. We'll just fit in that sucker. Where is it?"

"It's in a lot next to the garage."

"I'm there," Lula said. "Lead the way, and hurry up. I can feel bags growing under my eyes."

We followed Briggs to the lot and filed one by one after him into the RV.

"We can't turn too many lights on because no one's supposed to live here," Briggs said. "This is just a lot for hotel parking. I have a little battery-run lamp that I use."

Briggs switched the light on, and we all squinted into the dimly lit RV. It looked like at one time it had been a big, boxy Winnebago, but that was a while ago. It had been modified by exterior paint and patch and a complete interior retrofit.

"What the heck is this?" Lula said. "Everything's teeny tiny. Look at this itty-bitty chair. It looks like dollhouse furniture. How am I supposed to get my ass in this chair?"

"This RV was owned by a little person," Briggs said. "It fits me perfect."

"I feel like I'm in Barbie's camper," Lula said. "Where are we supposed to sleep?"

"There's the couch here in the front, and then there's two bunks in the middle of the RV, and there's a bedroom in the back with a double bed. That's where I sleep."

"The heck it is," Lula said. "Do you have a photo shoot in the morning? Hell, no. Get outta my way." Lula bustled into the bedroom and slammed the door shut.

Diesel looked at the bunks. "These are only four feet long."

"Plenty of room for me," Briggs said, rolling into the bottom bunk, pulling his curtain closed.

Snuggy looked at the top bunk. "I guess I could just about fit." He climbed the ladder, settled in, and closed his curtain.

Diesel was hands on hips. "That leaves the couch for us, Sweet Thing."

"The couch is five feet long and maybe a foot and a half wide. Your shoulders are wider than that."

Diesel kicked his shoes off and stretched out on the couch, one knee bent, one foot on the floor. "You can have the top."

"You're kidding!"

"Do I look like I'm kidding?"

I shut the light off, got rid of the sneakers and leather jacket, and maneuvered myself onto Diesel, breast to chest, my knee wedged between his legs. "Am I squishing you?"

Diesel wrapped his arms around me. "No, but it'd be good if you don't make any fast moves with the knee."

"Oh, cripes," Briggs said from his bunk. "You two aren't gonna get romantic out there, are you? This is a family RV."

"If I thought there was a chance for romance, I wouldn't be worrying about her knee," Diesel said.

6

I was jolted out of a sound sleep. Without thinking, I tried to roll over, and Diesel and I fell off the couch and crashed to the floor.

Diesel was halfway on top of me. "Earthquake," he murmured. "Where am I? Thailand? Japan?"

"Atlantic City."

"Am I drunk?"

"No. You were holding on to me, and I rolled us off the couch."

The door to the bedroom burst open, and Lula stormed out in the gold supermodel outfit. "What time is it? Am I late? Did I oversleep?"

Diesel checked his watch. "It's six-thirty."

"I'm supposed to be at the photo shoot first thing in the morning. What does **first thing in the morning** mean?"

I dragged myself up to my feet and realized I was still in the little SWEET THING T-shirt, but I wasn't wearing a bra. "What the heck?" I said, looking down at myself.

Diesel pulled my bra out of his back pocket. "You were uncomfortable."

"How did my bra get off my body and into your back pocket?"

"One of my many special talents," Diesel said, handing the bra over to me.

"I gotta go," Lula said. "I got a room number where I'm supposed to show up, and I'm just gonna go wait."

Briggs stuck his head out of his bunk. "It's the middle of the night, for crissake. I'm trying to sleep here. Do you mind?"

Diesel sat on the couch to lace his

boots. "I'm hungry. I'm going in search of breakfast."

"I'm going to get dressed and then check on Grandma," I said. "I'll meet you at the café."

I was back to wearing my sweatshirt and V-neck sweater, and I was in front of Grandma's door. Grandma was usually an early riser, but just in case, I'd taken the keycard from Briggs. I knocked once. No answer. I knocked again and was about to insert the keycard in the lock when the door opened. A guy reached out, grabbed me, and yanked me into the room.

I recognized the guy. Wheelman for Lou Delvina. I didn't know the guy's name, but he and Lou looked a lot alike. Early sixties and built like a fireplug. Lots of black hair and caterpillar eyebrows. He had the front of my sweatshirt in one hand and a gun in the other.

"This is good. Real convenient. Now we don't have to call you."

When something like this happens, adrenaline pours into your system. It's the whole fight-or-flight thing. It worked good back in caveman days because the smart choice was always flight, and you don't have to think a lot to run like hell. My reaction to the adrenaline is complete and utter panic. I break out in a sweat. My heart goes nuts. My mind freezes. Fortunately, it only lasts for a minute or two, and when the panic leaves, I go into survival mode.

"I can see you're real surprised," he said. "Probably you don't remember me. I'm Mickey. I work for Mr. Delvina. We had a run-in with you not so long ago."

"I remember."

"Then you must remember Mr. Delvina," Mickey said.

A gray blob of a creature hobbled in from the bedroom. "Well, well, Stephanie

Plum," the creature said. The voice was deep and croaky. The face was puffed up, the bloated body oozed into the head so that no neck was visible. The eyes bulged.

"Lou Delvina?" I asked, not entirely successful at hiding the shock. Last I saw him he was an ordinary middle-aged Italian man. And now he was . . . a giant toad.

"Funny how things work out. I get money stolen from me, and it brings me **you.** Drops you right in my lap. How lucky is that? Bad luck brings good luck."

"Are you sure you're Lou Delvina?"

"Mr. Delvina hadda take steroids for a rash. He got some water retention," Mickey said.

"Where's Grandma?"

"She's in the other room. We were just getting ready to take her for a ride. We stopped in to see if she wanted to give us our money, but she said she didn't have it."

"It's in the hotel safe."

"That's just what she said. And she said she couldn't get it out of the safe."

"I hear you talking about me, you nitwit," Grandma yelled from the other room. "What part of **I can't get it out of the safe** don't you understand?"

"It's true," I said. "She can't get it out because she didn't put it in. I put it in."

"That's a big fib," Mickey said. "I called down to the desk. Some guy named Randy Briggs put it in."

"He was a real A-hole when he called," Grandma said from the bedroom. "He told them I was senile and couldn't remember. He's gonna go straight to heck."

"In case you're wondering, we got her restrained in the bedroom," Mickey said. "She's a nasty one. She kicked me in the knee. We weren't even doing nothing to her."

"I was aiming for your privates," Grandma said, "but I couldn't get my leg up high enough."

"You see what I mean?" Mickey said. "How's that for an old lady to talk?"

Lou Delvina motioned for Mickey to bring Grandma out of the bedroom. "Bring her out," he said. "I got things to do. I gotta get back to Trenton. I'm due for my allergy shot."

Mickey trotted into the bedroom and wheeled Grandma out. They had her tied to a wheelchair and covered with a blanket.

"Pretty good, hunh?" Mickey said. "No one will know we're kidnapping her. Lots of old ladies getting rolled around this place."

Delvina shook his finger at Grandma. "You better be good when we get you out of this room. You make a fuss, and Mickey's gonna give you a blast with the stun gun, make you piss your pants."

"That don't scare me," Grandma said. "You get to be my age, and you do that all the time."

"Why are you kidnapping her?" I asked Delvina.

"I want my money."

"You already have a horse. How many hostages do you need?"

"As many as it takes."

"Take me instead of Grandma. I'll be more cooperative."

"You tricked me and Mickey last time we saw you," Delvina said. "I didn't like that. You and that train engine guy . . . Diesel." Some color came into Delvina's swollen, blotchy face. "I hate him. And you'll see, my time's gonna come. You don't mess with Lou Delvina. I got where I am today because I'm tough. I hold a grudge, and I get even. Everyone knows that. And now I got a plan. Ain't that right, Mickey?"

"Yeah, boss, you got a plan."

"What kind of plan?" I asked him.

"A **big** plan."

Oh boy. Besides looking like a toad, Lou Delvina had gone a little nutso.

"The first part of the plan is that I want my money," Delvina croaked. "Get the money to me, and you get your granny back."

"Why don't you wait here, and I'll get the money. I just have to find Briggs."

"What, do I look stupid?" Delvina said. "You'll come back with the cops. And besides, I gotta get my shot. And Mickey's gotta feed the horse."

Mickey was still holding his gun on me. He handed the gun to Delvina and took cuffs from his back pocket. "Gimme your wrist," Mickey said.

"No."

"Give it to me, or Lou's gonna shoot."

"I don't think he'll shoot me."

"You got that right," Delvina said. "I'll

shoot the old lady. I'd **love** to shoot the old lady."

I blew out a sigh and held my hand out for Mickey to cuff. He snapped a cuff on, walked me into the bathroom, and attached the other bracelet to the towel bar.

Mickey left the bathroom, closing the door after him. Seconds later, I heard the faint sound of the door to the suite opening and closing.

On the surface, Lou Delvina and Mickey were clichéd, mid-level, bumbling bad guys right out of central casting for every Mob movie ever made. At least, they used to be before Delvina's cortisone issue. Problem was, Delvina was right about his reputation. Delvina had ruthlessly scratched and clawed his way up the crime ladder in Newark and finally had been rewarded with his own piece of real estate. That real estate was Trenton. In the old days, it would have been a prize, but the old days were gone and the Mob no longer exclusively ran Trenton. The Mob had to share the Trenton pie with Russian thugs, kid gangs, Asian triads, black and Hispanic gangstas. So Delvina was still scratching and clawing, and sometimes people who got in his way disappeared.

I sat on the edge of the tub and waited. Eventually, someone would show up. A maid. Diesel. Briggs. A half hour ground by and I heard my phone ringing in my purse in the other room. I prayed it wasn't my mother. My mother was going to freak. She sent me out to retrieve Grandma Mazur and now Grandma was kidnapped.

The phone stopped ringing and I waited some more. Ten minutes later, I heard someone enter the suite.

"Help," I yelled. "I'm locked in the bathroom."

Diesel opened the door and looked in at

me. "I'm not usually into bondage, but I'm getting turned on."

"Delvina and his pal Mickey were here. They kidnapped Grandma."

"Is that a bad thing?"

"Yes!"

Diesel pulled his keyring from his pocket, sorted through his keys, plugged one into the cuff, and the cuff opened.

"I thought you'd magically make the cuff fall off my wrist," I said to him.

"I could, but that would be showing off."

"Delvina is taking Grandma back to Trenton and holding her hostage for the money . . . along with the horse."

"Delvina's beginning to annoy me," Diesel said.

"Last time he annoyed you, you threatened to turn him into a toad. And now his voice is croaky and he's fat and blobby and has no neck."

"Imagine that."

"You didn't turn Delvina into a toad, did you?"

Diesel smiled. "He isn't really a toad. He's just toadlike."

"Sometimes you can be downright scary."

"Yeah, but I'm sexy and cuddly, so it's okay."

I hauled my cell phone out of my bag, and I called Briggs. It rang a bunch of times and went to his answering service.

"We need the money out of the vault," I said to Diesel. "I'm worried about Grandma Mazur. Delvina isn't a nice guy."

"Briggs is probably asleep," Diesel said. "We'll go to the RV and get him up."

I went through the suite and packed up Grandma's things so I could check her out when I got downstairs. I wanted to make sure she had no reason to come back.

———

Snuggy was at the built-in banquette when we entered the RV. He was eating cereal, and he was looking rumpled.

"This sucks," Snuggy said. "I haven't got any clean clothes. I haven't even got a toothbrush. And there's no milk for the cereal."

"Where's Briggs? Is he still asleep?" I asked.

"No. His phone rang right after you left, and he got up and went out. I think he's got a thing going with some girl."

"Did he say anything? Do you know anything about the girl?"

"Nope. Didn't say anything."

The door banged open, and Lula stormed in.

"I'm gonna kill him," Lula said. "I'm gonna find him and kill him. And then I'm gonna kick the crap out of him. I been sitting outside this hotel room, wondering when this photo shoot was gonna start, and along comes a maid and goes into the room. So I go in with her and what do you think I see? They're gone. There's no one in the friggin' room. So I go down to the desk and ask where they are, and turns out they took off in the middle of the night."

Snuggy tapped the cereal box with his spoon. "Want some cereal?"

"Yeah," Lula said. "I didn't have breakfast. I could eat a horse. Nothing personal."

"I bet it was a scam," Snuggy said. "You pay the photographer money to make a portfolio, and then he doesn't even have film in the camera. Happens all the time."

"How do you know?"

"It was on **Everybody Loves Raymond**. Ray's brother got scammed like that."

Lula dumped a load of cereal into a bowl and started shoveling it into her mouth. "Wait a minute," Lula said. "There's no milk in this cereal."

"We haven't got any milk," I told her.

"I'm so mad, I don't know what I'm eating. I'm beside myself. I gotta take a breath. I gotta calm down. I'm probably giving myself a stroke." She scarfed down some more cereal. "So what's happening around here? I miss anything while I was getting scammed?"

"Lou Delvina kidnapped Grandma."

"Get out! Why'd he want to do that?"

"He figured we didn't want the horse back bad enough, so he took another hostage."

"He took the wrong one," Lula said. "No offense. I like your grandma and all, but she's gonna make their life a living hell."

That was my fear. If Grandma got too cantankerous, Delvina might think she wasn't worth the effort and get rid of her . . . permanently.

Diesel was slouched on the couch. "How did Delvina find Grandma?" he asked Snuggy.

"It wasn't me," Snuggy said. "I swear."

Diesel kept looking at him. Not saying anything. Just looking.

Snuggy squirmed in his seat. "He must have followed me here."

Now we were all looking at Snuggy.

"Okay!" Snuggy said. "He **did** follow me. I saw him. I didn't have a choice. He was gonna kill Doug, and he had me by the short hairs. And I figured it didn't matter that he was here. I figured he was just watching me. And then he started pressuring me, calling me, so I told him I couldn't get my hands on the money because it was in the vault. I didn't know he'd kidnap Grandma. He had Doug. Who'd think he'd kidnap an old woman?"

"I don't want to be an alarmist or anything," I said to Diesel, "but we need to get Grandma back **now**."

"We can bring the police in, but that would get messy for Snuggy and Doug. And Delvina might panic and make Grandma disappear."

I bit into my lower lip to keep from sniveling, and told myself to get a grip. I didn't want Grandma to disappear.

"Looks like we'll have to get the money without Briggs," Diesel said.

"Oh boy," Lula said. "Are we gonna rob the vault?"

"No," Diesel said. "We're going to help them return our deposit."

We took the elevator and followed Daffy's footprints through the casino gaming floor to hotel reception.

"I want to know the safety deposit box routine," Diesel said. "Someone needs to go to the desk and ask to get walked through the process."

"I'll do it," Lula said. "Us supermodels are always carrying a shitload of jewelry. I'll tell them I need to know everything's okay before I hand over my valuables for safekeeping. And if they disrespect me, I'll scream discrimination. It's illegal to discriminate against a supermodel. We got rights like everyone else."

Lula strutted up to the desk, and we all watched while she talked to one of the clerks. The clerk turned Lula over to a manager, and the manager led Lula into a back room. Ten minutes later, Lula emerged, thanked the manager and clerk, and crossed the lobby to where we were waiting.

"You gotta get behind the desk and through the door," Lula said. "Once you're through the door, you walk down the hall and take a special service elevator two flights down. It opens into another hallway with a guard at a desk. You gotta show the guard your ID and do one of them fingerprint scans like at Disney World. If I was by myself, I wouldn't have got anywhere, but I was with the manager, so he took me halfway down the hall to a

PLUM LUCKY   137

door marked GUESTS. That's the door that leads to the guest security boxes. There's other doors down there that lead to the money-counting room and all, but they're locked up tight. Once you get into the room with the security boxes, you can only open them with a key and a code. You get the code wrong, and the Marines come and cut your balls off. Oh yeah, and another thing, you're always on television," she said to Diesel, "so maybe you want to comb your hair."

"How do I know which box is mine?" Diesel asked.

"The guy at the desk with the fingerprint machine has a book with everyone's name and box number. Plus, did I tell you he's got a gun? A big one."

"The armed guard is a problem," Diesel said. "I can scramble television transmissions, and I can open locks. I can't make myself invisible."

"I got a stun gun," Lula said. "How about you jump out of the elevator and real quick you give him some jolts? You just gotta move fast before he shoots you. How fast can you move?"

"I can't move as fast as a bullet."

"I can get past the guard," Snuggy said. "I can be real sneaky when it comes to people. I have this thing. Take your eyes off me, and I disappear."

"I hear leprechauns can do that," Lula said.

"Exactly!" Snuggy said to her.

Diesel looked down at Snuggy. "You don't disappear. You have a knack for knowing when people are distracted."

"I'm almost positive I disappear," Snuggy said.

"If you're wrong, the Marines are gonna cut your balls off," Lula told him.

"I'd hate that," Snuggy said. "I'm attached to my balls."

Diesel scanned the lobby and looked

beyond it into the gaming area. "I wish Briggs would show up."

I dialed Briggs, and we all waited while his phone rang. Finally, his service kicked in.

"Call me!" I said. "**Now.**"

"Let's assume you can actually get past the guard," Diesel said to Snuggy. "Can you open the locked door to the safety deposit box room and get into the box?"

"Piece of cake. Problem is, I'll get caught by the security cameras. For some reason, television picks up my image."

"I can scramble the television," Diesel said, "but you can't waste time once you're out of the elevator. You'll only have a couple minutes before they send someone to investigate."

"I can do it," Snuggy said. "Doug is depending on me."

My phone rang, and I snatched it out of my pocket, hoping it was Briggs.

"Plum?"

It was Lou Delvina. Easy to recognize his croaky voice.

"You better be on the road with my money," Delvina said.

"Not yet, but I'm working on it."

"You have until three o'clock. First, I kill the horse, and then the old lady. And then I'll come get you. Or maybe I should go for your mother next. Or your sister. Or even better, one of your little nieces."

Delvina disconnected, and Diesel wrapped an arm around me. "Are you okay? Your face just went white."

"We need to get Delvina his money."

Diesel looked over at the registration desk and then at Snuggy. "I know I'm going to regret this," Diesel said.

"How do you want to do it?" Snuggy asked. "Do you want me to just slip behind the desk and go to the elevator?"

"No. I need to go to the elevator with

you. That means I need a diversion, so we're going to play some slots."

Ten minutes later, Lula had a bucket filled with quarters and nickels.

"I love when they have nickel slots," Lula said, two arms around the bucket. "I like seeing all that money drop into the tray. It don't matter that you only won eight dollars. It's the experience of the money coming out at you that counts. And I can't believe how lucky we were. I never was able to fill a bucket like this."

I cut my eyes to Diesel.

"I'm a lucky kind of guy," Diesel said.

"Maybe you're a leprechaun."

"It doesn't say leprechaun on my driver's license."

"Well, if anyone would know, it would be the DMV."

"Okay, let's do it," Diesel said. "This is how it's going to go down. Stephanie stays here, so we have someone to float bail if we all get arrested. Snuggy stays glued to my side until I get the communications scrambled. And Lula creates chaos, so Snuggy and I can get behind the desk."

"I get it," Lula said. "You want me to dump the bucket."

"Exactly," Diesel said. "Make sure all eyes are on you."

Lula shrugged out of the black jacket and handed it over. "Leave it to me. You have to be dead not to be looking at me do this. I'm gonna be the Queen of Chaos."

Lula minced up to the desk in her stiletto heels and skintight gold-sequined supermodel outfit. The skirt was three inches below her ass, and her boobs moved like Jell-O barely held in place by the bustier. She held the bucket of change at arm's length in front of her, not wanting to distract from her natural assets.

"Yoohoo!" she called to one of the men behind the registration desk. "I'm almost a supermodel, and I've got a bucket full of money. I'm thinking I might need some help protecting all this money. I'm thinking . . . whoops!" Lula stumbled, jerked the bucket, and the money shot out in all directions. "My money!" Lula shrieked.

Lula bent to retrieve her money, and her left boob fell out of the top and her skirt rode up past the full moon. She was wearing a matching gold thong, but most of the thong was lost in deep space. The entire hotel and casino gasped. It was as if all the air instantly got sucked in and, seconds later, got spewed out. Four guards rushed to the scene, and all six men behind the registration desk were mouths agape, eyes glued to Lula.

Lula stood and pushed her boob back into the top of her dress and pulled her skirt down. Then she bent in another direction to get her money, and the boob fell out again, and the dress rode up. People were scrambling around her, trying to scoop up the change and return it to the bucket without unduly sticking their noses in Lula's business. And Lula kept spilling the money out of the bucket and bending over.

"My word," Lula exclaimed. "Mercy me! Lordy, Lordy, Lordy."

Diesel and Snuggy disappeared behind the door that led to the elevator, and Lula continued to create chaos. She was finally stopped by an assistant manager, who grabbed the bucket. Most of the change was returned to the bucket, and the manager asked Lula if she would like the change converted into paper money or Daffy Dollars.

"Do you think I should?" Lula asked him. "What would you do? Maybe I should just take this and keep playing. I think I'm hot. Don't I look hot?" Lula looked over at me. "What do you think I should do?"

I was watching the door behind the desk. Fifteen minutes had passed. Briggs had returned in ten when he got Diesel's poker stake.

"I think you should put it back in the machine," I said. "And save some for parking meters."

The door opened and Diesel ambled out. He was stopped by one of the registration people. He swayed a little and smiled. Snatches of conversation carried across the floor.

"Lookin' for the can," Diesel said. "They said it was in there, but I couldn't find it. There should be signs, right? How'r people supposed to know?"

"Public restrooms are across the lobby," Diesel was told.

"Okay," Diesel said, and he wandered

toward me, a little unsteady on his feet. He reached Lula, and the door behind the desk banged open, and Snuggy came flying out. Snuggy was moving so fast his legs were a green blur. The guard chasing after him was slow by comparison, overweight and breathing hard.

Diesel bumped into Lula and knocked the bucket out of her hands. For the second time, people scurried for the money like roaches on pie. The guard pulled up, unsure of Snuggy's direction, craning his neck, attempting to see around the gathering crowd.

"I'll give ya ten dollars to do me in the lot," Diesel said to Lula.

"I'm there," Lula said. "Excuse me," she said to the manager. "I got business."

We all power walked through the casino and broke into a run when we reached the lot. Snuggy was already in the RV with the engine cranked over when we tumbled in.

"Go," Diesel said to Snuggy. "And don't look back."

A half hour later, we were on the Garden State Parkway heading for Trenton, and my heart rate was almost normal.

"What the heck was that back there?" Lula wanted to know.

Diesel was sprawled on the couch. "I was able to scramble the feed, but just to be safe I went down in the elevator with Mr. Sneaky. What happened after that is classic Snuggy O'Connor.

"The elevator doors opened, Snuggy zipped out and went straight to the guard at the desk and started thumbing through the guy's logbook, looking for the box number. 'What the hell do you think you're doing?' the guard says. 'And where did you come from? Where's your ID?' So Snuggy says, 'You can't see me. I'm a leprechaun.'"

"I could have sworn I disappeared," Snuggy said, concentrating, keeping his eyes on the road while he drove.

"But he wasn't disappeared?" Lula guessed.

"Not even a little," Diesel said. "The guard pulled his gun and pointed it at Snuggy's forehead."

"I don't understand why it didn't work," Snuggy said. "It always worked before."

"Maybe it didn't work because you aren't a friggin' leprechaun," Diesel said.

"Did you get the money?" I asked.

"Yeah," Diesel said. "I persuaded the guard to go to sleep, and we got the money. And then Green Pants panicked when a second guard came in. He took off shrieking like a girl and ran all the hell over the building with the guard running after him."

My phone rang, and I grimaced at the number displayed. It was my mother.

"I'm calling the police," my mother said. "Where are you?"

"I'm on my way back to Trenton."

"Thank goodness. Let me talk to your grandmother."

"She's sleeping."

"It's morning. How could she be sleeping?"

"I don't know, but I'm pretty sure she's sleeping."

"Will you be home soon?" my mother asked. "I have cold cuts for lunch. Should I make some potato salad? Maybe get some nice rolls."

"Grandma said she wanted to go shopping, so we won't be home for lunch. I'm going to take her to Quaker Bridge Mall." I made some static sounds. "I'm breaking up," I yelled into the phone. "Can't hear you. Gotta go." And I disconnected.

Diesel was smiling. "You're going straight to hell for lying to your mother."

"You never lied to your mother?"

"I'm a guy. It's expected."

"What's the plan when we hit Trenton?"

Snuggy wanted to know. "Where am I supposed to park this monster?"

"Drop Lula and me at the bonds office on Hamilton, so we can get our cars. Then you can park this in the lot behind my apartment building," I said.

7

Lula and I watched the RV pull away from the curb and chug down Hamilton.

"This has been a strange couple days," Lula said. "Good luck and bad luck and good luck and bad luck. And then there's the stupid leprechaun. And now your grandma's been kidnapped. How often does that happen? 'Course, there was that time she got locked up in the casket and burned the funeral home down. I guess that counts for a kidnap."

I was fishing through my purse, searching for my car keys. "I'm worried about her. Delvina is a scary guy."

"Tell you the truth, I'm worried about her, too. Is there anything I can do?"

"No, but thanks. You were great today."

"I'm going inside to talk to Connie." She looked past me to the car pulling up to the curb. "You have a visitor. Mr. Tall, Hot, and Handsome is here."

Ranger parked his black Porsche Turbo and angled out of the car. He was in his usual Rangeman black. Black boots, black cargo pants that fit perfectly across his butt, black T-shirt under a black windbreaker with RANGEMAN written in black on the sleeve. He walked over and gave me a friendly, lingering kiss on my temple, just above my ear.

"Babe."

Babe covered a lot of ground with Ranger. Depending on the inflection, it could be sexy, scolding, or wistful. He said "babe" when I amused him, astonished him, and exasperated him. Today, it was mostly hello.

He gave my ponytail a playful tug. "You look worried."

"I could use some help. Lou Delvina kidnapped Grandma."

"When did this happen?"

"This morning. Two days ago, on St. Patrick's Day, Grandma found a bag of money. She bought an RV and hired Randy Briggs to drive her to Atlantic City. Turns out, the money belonged to this little guy who thinks he's a leprechaun. And the leprechaun stole the money from Delvina. So Delvina kidnapped the leprechaun's horse and Grandma until he gets his money. Problem is, we only have **some** of his money."

"We?"

"Diesel and me."

Ranger covered his face with his hands, pressing his fingertips against his eyes. It was one of those gestures you do instead of jumping off a bridge or choking someone. "Diesel," Ranger said.

"He's not your favorite person?"

"We don't hang out together."

"I think he turned Delvina into a toad."

"Delvina only looks like a toad. Under the warts, he's still a middle-aged, mid-level mobster. And he's ruthless. And a little insane."

"Great. This makes me feel much better."

"You haven't gone to the police?"

"No."

"Morelli?"

"No. We were afraid Delvina would panic and make Grandma disappear."

"That's a genuine concern," Ranger said. "How can I help you?"

"For starters, you can get me Delvina's phone number."

Ranger called his office and asked for Delvina's number. Moments later, he gave it to me. "Now what?" he asked.

"Hopefully, this will do it. I'll give him his money, and he'll give me Grandma."

"Call me if there are complications. I have to run. I need to look in on a commercial account."

I immediately called Delvina. "Okay," I said, "I have the money." Most of it. "How do you want to do this?"

"Put the duffel bag on the passenger seat of a car and take the car to the car wash at three o'clock. If the money's all there, you'll get your grandmother."

"Will she be at the car wash?"

"More or less. We'll deliver her to the car wash as soon as we count the money. You shouldn't worry about it. Trust me, the sooner we're rid of her, the better."

"I suppose I should tell you we're a little short."

"How short?"

"Roughly . . . a hundred and forty thousand, more or less."

"No deal. No way. I need all the money. At three o'clock, we shoot the horse, and then we shoot the old lady. I'm almost hoping you don't get the money. I really want to shoot the old lady."

I got into my piece-of-crap car and drove to my apartment building. By the time I got there, I'd sort of stopped crying. I ran up the stairs and took a minute to blow my nose and get myself under control before I opened the door.

Snuggy was on the couch, watching television. He was looking more like Dublin bum than leprechaun.

"Where do you keep all your green pants?" I asked him. "Do you live near here?"

"I have an apartment in Hamilton Township. By the pet cemetery."

That figured.

Diesel strolled out of my bedroom wearing his same clothes but looking fresh out of the shower. His hair was still damp and the stubble was gone.

"I used your razor and toothbrush," Diesel said. "I figured you wouldn't mind."

"You aren't diseased, are you?"

"I couldn't get a disease if I tried." He stood for a beat with his thumbs hooked into his pants pockets. "Are you okay?"

"Yes." A tear leaked out of my eye and streaked down my cheek.

"Oh, shit," Diesel said. "I'm not good at this. It's not the toothbrush, is it? I'll buy you a new one."

"It's Grandma. He's going to shoot her because we haven't got all the money. I talked to him, and he told me they were going to count the money, and if it wasn't all there, they were going to shoot Grandma and the horse."

"So we have to get more money," Snuggy said. "How hard can it be?"

"We're not talking about small change," Diesel said. "We need a hundred and forty thousand dollars."

"Maybe you could pop into a bank," Snuggy said to Diesel.

Diesel looked at his watch. "Delvina's

keeping the horse and the woman somewhere. Let's see if we can find them. If we
can't find them by two o'clock, we'll go to
plan B."

"What's plan B?" I asked him.

"I don't actually have a plan B. I suppose plan B would involve the police. I'm
going to have Flash take a look at Delvina's country house."

Flash works with Diesel. Or maybe
Flash works **for** Diesel. Or maybe Flash is
just Diesel's friend. Hard to tell where
Flash fits in the big picture. He's slim and
spikey-haired and a couple inches taller
than me. He lives in Trenton. He has a
girlfriend. He likes to ski. And he's a
handy guy to have on your team. That's
everything I know about Flash.

Diesel punched Flash's number into his
phone. "I need you to check out Lou
Delvina's house in Bucks County," he said
when the connection was made. "He's
holding a horse and Stephanie's grand-

mother as hostages somewhere. I'm going to scope out his house in Trenton."

"Is there something I can do?" Snuggy asked.

"You can stay here and not make a move," Diesel said. "When we leave, don't open the door to anyone. Don't order pizza. Don't buy Girl Scout cookies. Don't look out a window. Bolt the door and keep the television low." Diesel had his head in the refrigerator. "There's nothing in here. How can you live without food?"

"I have peanut butter in the cupboard and some crackers."

"I like peanut butter and crackers," Snuggy said.

"Knock yourself out," Diesel said. He wrapped an arm around me. "Let's hustle. I want to see the car wash, and then we'll snoop around Delvina's social club. He has a house in Cranbury, but I don't think he'd keep a horse and an old lady locked up with his wife."

I followed Diesel down the stairs, through the small lobby, and out the back door. We got to the car, and he took the keys from me.

"Excuse me?" I said.

"I'll drive."

"I don't think so. This is my car, and I drive."

"The guy drives. Everyone knows that."

"Only in Saudi Arabia."

He dangled the keys over my head. "Do you think you can get these keys from me?"

"Do you think you can walk after I kick you in the knee?"

"You can be a real pain in the ass," Diesel said.

Another tear slid down my cheek.

"You forced yourself to do that," Diesel said.

"I didn't. I'm feeling very emotional. I'm hungry and I need a shower and some awful toad man is going to shoot my grandmother. And I'm tired. I didn't get a lot of sleep last night."

"It was nice last night," Diesel said. "I liked holding you."

"You're trying to soften me up."

"Is it working?"

I did some mental eye rolling and got into the passenger side of the car.

The car wash wasn't far from my apartment. We cruised past, made a U-turn, and drove by a second time. It was a little after eleven o'clock on a Thursday, and the car wash was empty. Three Hispanic guys in car wash gear lounged in front of the drive-through brushless system that was built into a cement block tunnel. The waiting room and Delvina's office were a couple feet away in a second cement block building. The waiting room was glass-fronted, and I could see some vending machines and a counter with a cash register, but no people. There were two junker cars in the lot. Nothing that looked like it would belong to Delvina.

Diesel drove around a couple blocks, getting the lay of the land, looking for black Mafia staff cars. We didn't see any Mafia cars, horse barns, hay wagons, or men hobbling around holding their privates because Grandma finally managed to get her leg up high enough to do damage.

"Delvina could have your grandmother stashed anywhere," Diesel said. "The horse is a whole other thing. You don't ride a horse through downtown Trenton to get handed off for ransom. Delvina needs a horse van to move Doug around. So far, I'm not seeing any evidence of a horse or a van."

Diesel turned onto Roebling and slowed when he came to Delvina's social club. It was a dingy, redbrick, two-story row house. Two metal folding chairs from Lugio's Funeral Home had been placed beside the front stoop. This was Chambersburg patio furniture. Pottery Barn, eat your heart out. There was no visible activity in or around the club. No place to hide a horse.

Diesel took the alley behind the row houses. Each house had a small, narrow yard with a single-car garage at the rear. Diesel parked halfway down the alley, left the car, and walked. He looked in each of the garages and in all the yards.

"No sign of a horse," he said when he returned. "But I'm guessing a couple people are hijacking trucks. Do you need a toaster?"

I called Connie and asked if Delvina had any other properties.

"Hold on," Connie said. "I'll run him through some programs."

I listened to Connie tap onto her computer keyboard and waited while she read through information appearing on her screen.

"So far, I'm only showing his house in Cranbury and his house in Bucks County. Plus the car wash. I know he owns other properties, but they were probably bought through a holding company. I can run that down, but it'll take a while. I'll call you back."

"Thanks."

"We have time," Diesel said. "We might as well look at the house in Cranbury."

Cranbury is a pretty little town within shouting distance of Route 130. Delvina lived on a quiet, tree-lined street. His house was white clapboard with black shutters and a red door. It was two stories, with a two-car detached garage. The lot was maybe a quarter acre and filled with trees and flowerbeds and shrubs. Mrs. Delvina liked to garden.

"This all seems so benign, so normal,"

Diesel said, sitting in the car, looking across the street at the house.

"Maybe when Delvina is in this house he **is** sort of normal."

Diesel methodically drove up and down streets in Delvina's neighborhood. There were some rural areas around Cranbury where a horse could be kept without notice, but we didn't know where to begin.

I called Connie for a property update.

"I'm not finding anything local," Connie said. "He's got real estate in the Caymans and a condo in Miami under LD Sons Import."

"Did you try his wife's maiden name?"

"Yeah. Nothing came up."

Diesel put the Monte Carlo into gear and headed out of town, back to Trenton. We were on Broad Street when Flash called. I gave Diesel raised eyebrows, and he shook his head no. No sign of Grandma or Doug in Bucks County.

"I could use a change of clothes," Diesel told Flash. "And check to see if the O'Connor mess has been resolved. If it hasn't been resolved and I need to keep him close, he's going to need clothes, too. And a toothbrush."

We stopped at Cluck-in-a-Bucket, got bags of food, and brought them back to my apartment.

Snuggy was still on the couch in front of the television. We dumped the food on the coffee table and we all dug in.

"I got an idea while you were gone," Snuggy said. "Delvina won't give us Grandma, because we don't have all the money, but maybe he'll take the money we've got in exchange for Doug. We can ask for another twenty-four hours to come up with the rest. And here's the best part. Once we get hold of Doug, I can ask him where Delvina is keeping Grandma."

Diesel was halfway into a second

chicken sandwich. "On the surface, that sounds like an okay idea. If it turns out you can't actually talk to that horse, I'll throw you off the Route 1 bridge into the Delaware River."

"You have trust issues," Snuggy said to Diesel. "I sense some passive-aggressive tendencies."

"I'm not passive-aggressive," Diesel said. "I'm actively aggressive. And I'd have to be an idiot to trust you. You're a nut."

"Should I call Delvina?" I asked Diesel.

"Yeah. At the very worst, it'll buy us some time."

I had the money in the duffel bag on the seat next to me. I eased the Monte Carlo up to the car wash and put it in park. I got out and a guy in a car wash uniform got in. The Monte was rolled through the car wash, and when it emerged on the opposite side, the guy got out holding the duffel bag. He walked over to me and gave me a piece of paper. "This is from Mr. Delvina. He said you'd know what to do."

Diesel and Snuggy were in the RV half a block away. I drove around the block and parked my clean Monte Carlo behind the RV. I got out, locked up, and climbed on board. Snuggy was at the wheel. He was the only one who could fit in the seat.

"Here's the address," I said to Snuggy. "It's south of town, off Broad. It's a light industrial park that's pretty much abandoned."

Ten minutes later, Snuggy maneuvered the RV into the parking lot of a small warehouse. Grass grew from cracks in the pavement and one of the front office windows was covered with a plywood slab. Diesel hopped out and stood still for a moment. I supposed he was taking some sort of cosmic temperature. He walked to a side door, and Snuggy and I hopped out of the RV and followed him.

Diesel opened the door, and we all peered into the dim interior. Something rustled in a far corner, and deep in shadow I could see the horse. He was tethered to a cinder block. He turned his head and looked at us and made a horse sound. Not a high-pitched whinny. This was more of a low snuffle.

"Doug!" Snuggy yelled. And he ran to the horse and threw his arms around the horse's neck.

Diesel and I approached the horse, and I could see why Snuggy was so taken. The animal was beautiful. His mane and tail were black and his coat was chestnut. He had large, soulful brown eyes and long lashes. And he was massive. Even in the dark warehouse, you could sense his power. It was a lot like standing next to Diesel.

We cut the rope away from the cinder block and led Doug through the warehouse to the parking lot.

"Are you sure this is going to work?" I asked Snuggy.

"Sure, it'll work," Snuggy said. "Doug's a real trouper—right, Doug?"

Doug looked at Snuggy with his huge horse eye.

"Just exactly how do you talk to him?" I asked Snuggy.

"It's sort of telepathic."

"Can he understand me?"

"Yep. See, that's the mistake people make. Everyone thinks just because animals can't talk means they can't understand."

I thought about Morelli's dog, Bob. I was pretty sure Bob didn't understand a damn thing.

"Go ahead," Snuggy said to Doug. "Give her a sign that you understand."

Doug blinked.

"See," Snuggy said. "Impressive, hunh?"

"That was it? A blink?"

"Oh man," Diesel said. "We are so fucked."

Doug moved to the side and stepped on Diesel's foot. Diesel gave him a shot to the shoulder and Doug moved over, off Diesel's foot.

"Okay," I said, "now that each of you has marked your territory on the fire hydrant, can we get on with it?"

"We brought the RV instead of your car because it has a tow hitch, but they didn't leave the horse trailer," Snuggy said. "I borrowed a horse trailer from a friend, and they took it when they took Doug, and it's not here."

"Maybe you can ride him back," Diesel said.

"I can't ride him back on the highway!" Snuggy said. "And anyway, he has a bad leg. It hurts when he walks on it too much."

We all looked down at Doug's leg. It had a bandage wrapped around it.

"Put him in the RV," Diesel said.

Snuggy and I did an openmouthed **What?**

Diesel was looking a quart down on patience. "Do you have any better ideas?"

Snuggy and I shook our heads. We didn't have any ideas.

"We're wasting time," Diesel said.

Snuggy took Doug's halter and led him over to the door of the RV. There were three steps going up, and the door opening looked maybe a half-inch wider than Doug's ass.

Doug planted his feet firm on the ground and gave Snuggy a look that I swear said **Are you insane?**

"Up you go," Snuggy said. "Into the RV."

Doug didn't budge.

Snuggy went into telepathic mode, nodding his head, looking sympathetic.

"I understand your concern," Snuggy said to Doug, "but you have nothing to worry about. You have to make a tight turn when you first get in, but then you'll have plenty of room."

More telepathy.

"**I'm** driving," Snuggy said to Doug.

Doug still didn't move.

"What are you talking about?" Snuggy said. "I'm a good driver. I brought you around the track to win at Freehold."

Doug rolled his eyes.

"I fell off **after** we won," Snuggy said. "And it had nothing to do with my driving. It was one of those freak things."

"How about this," Diesel said to Doug. "You get into the RV, or we leave you in the parking lot and don't come back."

Snuggy went in first, pulling on Doug's halter, and Diesel put his shoulder to Doug's butt. After a lot of swearing on Diesel's part, and a lot of nervous foot stamping on Doug's part, Doug got himself into the RV.

"Jeez," Snuggy said to Doug. "Quit your complaining. Look at Diesel. He doesn't fit in here, either, but he's making the best of it."

Doug turned his horse eye on Diesel, and I didn't think it looked friendly.

"Maybe you want to give Doug some room," I said to Diesel. "Maybe you want to go up front and hang with Snuggy."

8

It was four o'clock when we cruised into the lot to my building and parked the RV in the back, next to the Dumpster.

"We should get Doug out of the RV for a couple minutes," Snuggy said. "Let him stretch his legs and go potty."

The possibility that Doug might have to go potty got us all on our feet. We maneuvered Doug into the back bedroom, turned him around, and managed to get him out the door and down the steps. Snuggy walked Doug around in the lot, but apparently Doug didn't feel the need to do anything. I wasn't all that unhappy, because I didn't know how I was going to explain a load of horse shit in the parking lot.

"Ask him about Grandma," I said to Snuggy. "Does he know where she is?"

Here's the thing. I didn't entirely buy into the whole horse talk business, but a part of me wanted to believe. Not only did I want to believe for Grandma's sake, but I liked the idea that communication was possible between species. I also liked the idea that reindeer could fly, there was such a thing as the birthday cake diet, and, most of all, I wanted to go to heaven.

"What about it?" Snuggy said to Doug. "Un-hunh, un-hunh, un-hunh."

I looked up at Diesel. "Are you getting anything?"

"Yeah, a real strong desire to quit my job and go to bartending school."

"Doug says before they drove him to the warehouse, they had him outside, in a yard, and he was tied to a thing in the

ground, like a dog. He said it was humili-
ating. He doesn't know exactly where it
was, but he might be able to spot it if you
drive him around."

"That's a little vague," Diesel said.

"Doug thinks they might have
Grandma there because he heard a lot of
yelling, and then they pulled the shades
down, so he couldn't see in the window.
And he thinks he might have heard a
gunshot."

"No!" I had my hand to my heart.
"When?"

"Just before they loaded him into the
horse trailer."

I whipped my phone out and dialed
Delvina.

"What?" Delvina said.

"Is my grandmother all right?"

"Was she ever all right?"

"I want to talk to her," I told him.

"No way. We got her locked in the crap-
per, and I'm not opening that door until I

get a cattle prod. Do you have the rest of my money?"

"Not yet, but I'm working on it."

Delvina disconnected.

"Doug says he's hungry," Snuggy said. "He said he had to eat grass, and there wasn't hardly any. He says he thinks he could be more helpful if he wasn't hungry."

Diesel dialed Flash. "I need horse food," he said to Flash. He listened a minute and studied his shoe. "I don't know what horses eat. Just go to a horse food store and let them figure it out. And bring some beer and pizza with the horse food."

"What are you going to do with Doug?" I asked Snuggy. "He needs a barn or a stable or something."

"I have him scheduled for surgery next week, and after that, I have a place for him to live in Hunterdon County. I just don't have anything for him right now. And I guess I'm in a bind with the surgery. I lost the money I was going to use."

I called my mother.

"Do you know anything about Lou Delvina?"

"You aren't involved with him, are you? He's a terrible person. If your cousin gave Delvina to you to find, you give him back. Let someone else look for him."

"He's not one of my cases. This is something else."

"Well, I hear he's sick. And something happened with him and his wife, because he's not living at the Cranbury house anymore."

"Do you know where he **is** living?"

"No, but I ran into Louise Kulach at church last week, and she said twice she saw Delvina getting cold cuts at the deli on Cherry Street. She said he looked terrible. She said you wouldn't recognize him, except the butcher told her who it was. Where's your grandmother?"

"She's in the bathroom."

"What should I do about supper? I have a pot of spaghetti sauce on the stove."

"Grandma wants to eat at the mall."

"I guess that's okay, but don't let her eat from that Chinese place. It always gives her the runs."

I put my phone back into my pocket. "North Trenton," I said to Diesel. "Delvina's been seen at the deli on Cherry Street."

"Never underestimate the value of gossip," Diesel said. "Let's roll before it gets dark."

"What about the horse food?" Snuggy asked.

"We'll stop at Cluck-in-a-Bucket," Diesel said.

"Doug doesn't eat burgers," Snuggy said. "Horses are vegetarians."

"Whatever," Diesel said. "We'll stop at

a supermarket and get him a head of lettuce. Just get him into the RV."

Snuggy rolled the RV slowly down Cherry Street. Doug was in the aisle between the dinette table and the couch, looking out the big front window, eating an apple. It was his fourth apple, and half the apple fell out of his mouth while he chewed. Turns out it's hard to eat an apple efficiently without opposable thumbs. We'd been driving a grid pattern through north Trenton, and this was our second pass down Cherry.

Diesel was perched on the seat next to Snuggy. "You'd better not be blowing smoke up my skirt with this horse," Diesel said to Snuggy.

Doug reached forward and bit Diesel on the shoulder. Not hard enough to draw blood, but hard enough to leave a dent and apple slobber on Diesel's shirt.

"This is the reason I don't carry a gun," Diesel said. "It'd be satisfying to shoot him, but I'd probably regret it . . . eventually."

Snuggy turned off Cherry, drove a couple blocks, and stopped in the middle of the road. "Doug says the neighborhood didn't look like this. He said the house was by itself."

"Was it in the woods? In the middle of a field?" I asked.

"No. It was just by itself," Snuggy said. "And it was noisy. He could hear cars all night long."

"Route 1," I said to Diesel. "The house was at the end of a street that backed up to Route 1."

The sun was setting, and I could see a rosy glow in the sky in front of us.

"Pretty sunset," I said.

"That's not a sunset," Diesel said. "The sun is behind us. That's a fire."

A cop car raced past us, and I heard sirens in the distance. Snuggy moved to the side of the road to allow a fire truck to get through.

"I've got a bad feeling about this," Diesel said. "Follow the truck."

Snuggy eased the RV down the street and parked a block from the fire. Cop cars and fire trucks were angled in front of the burning house. The house was at the end of a cul-de-sac. The lot was large. There was a two-car garage attached to the house. The garage doors were open and whatever was in the garage was on fire. Firemen were running hoses and shouting instructions to each other. There were large trees to the side and behind the house. The rumble of the fire trucks drowned out all other noise, but I knew on a quieter night you could hear the Route 1 traffic from here.

Diesel was on his feet. "Stay here," he said. "I'm going to look around."

"No way," I said. "I'm coming with you."

"Every cop and fireman in the county knows you," Diesel said. "Morelli will get a phone call, and we'll have the police involved in this."

"Maybe the police **should** be involved."

"Let me scope it out before we jump to conclusions. I'll be right back."

I sat on the couch and dialed Delvina. My hands were shaking, and I had to dial twice to get the right number. Delvina didn't answer.

My next call was to Connie. "Are you at the office or has this been forwarded?" I asked her.

"I'm still here. I'm trying to clear out some backed-up paperwork."

"I need you to run an address for me."

Moments later, she was back on the line. "The house is owned by Mickey Wallens, Delvina's wheelman."

I disconnected and clamped my teeth down into my lower lip. Snuggy and Doug were silent, watching out the front window with me. The three of us barely breathing. Diesel appeared from behind a fire truck and jogged back to the RV.

"It looks like the fire was started in a second-floor bathroom. The firefighters haven't determined if anyone was in the house, but I think the house was empty. One of the garage bays was empty. There was a horse trailer in the other. The horse trailer is toast."

"Now what?" Snuggy asked.

"Take us back to Stephanie's apartment," Diesel said.

"Drive by the car wash on the way," I told him. "I want to get my car."

Snuggy parked the RV in his spot by the Dumpster, and I parked one row up, making sure I could drive straight out. I got out of my car and tried Delvina one more time. The phone rang twice and he answered.

"Sonovabitch," he said.

"I want to talk to my grandmother."

"She's in the trunk. Don't worry about her. She's got a quilt and a pillow, and she's curled up next to the spare tire. It's a big trunk."

"She's old. That's awful!"

"I'll tell you what's awful. She burned Mickey's house down. She said it smelled like poop in the bathroom, so Mickey slid some matches to her under the door."

I could hear Mickey next to Delvina. "I was trying to be helpful."

"How many times I have to tell you," Delvina said to Mickey. "No guns, sharp objects, or matches to hostages."

"We never had a old lady hostage before," Mickey said. "I didn't know the rules was the same."

Delvina came back on the line to me. "So Sir Walter Raleigh here gives your grandma matches and she uses them to set off the smoke detector. Then somehow the curtains got caught on fire. We're lucky we didn't die, for crissake. Now we're riding around like some homeless people. I gotta go. I think we're lost."

Delvina disconnected.

"Well?" Diesel said.

"They're lost."

"I know the feeling," Diesel said. "I'm going upstairs, where I hope there's some pizza and beer waiting for me."

We all walked over to the back door, and when I reached it, I realized Doug had followed us.

"What are we going to do with Doug?" I said.

"Doug can stay in the RV," Diesel said.

"Doug doesn't want to stay in the RV," Snuggy said. "He's freaked out from the fire. Doug wants to stay with us."

"Yeah, but this is an apartment building for people," I said.

"Doesn't it allow pets?"

"Not horses!"

"How do you know? Does it say that in your rental agreement? And anyway, you let Diesel stay here."

"Diesel is housebroken."

"So is Doug," Snuggy said.

Doug was standing with his head down, looking pathetic, not putting any weight on his bad leg.

"Oh, for goodness sakes," I said.

Snuggy, Diesel, Doug, and I got into the elevator, and I looked at the posted weight limit.

"How much does Doug weigh?" I asked Snuggy.

"About thirteen hundred pounds," Snuggy said. "Don't anyone breathe. I'm going to push the button. We only have to go up one floor."

The elevator paused when it got to the second floor, and I prayed that the doors would open. I didn't want to get caught in an elevator with a horse. The doors opened after a long moment, and we all paraded down the hall to my apartment. Flash had left a sack of grain, two buckets, two six-packs of beer, three pizzas, and a duffel bag with Diesel's and Snuggy's clothes in front of my door.

We carried everything inside and closed and locked the door. Snuggy poured some grain into a bucket for Doug and filled the second bucket with water. Diesel took one of the pizza boxes and a beer and settled himself in front of the television.

Some people can't eat when they're under stress. I get hungry when I'm nervous. I eat to fill the hollow feeling in my stomach. I sat next to Diesel and wolfed down pizza. I looked at the box and saw that it was empty.

"Are you going to eat the cardboard, too?" Diesel asked.

"Did I eat pizza?"

"Four pieces."

"I don't remember."

"Take a deep breath," Diesel said. He

put his hands on my shoulders and kneaded. "Keep breathing," he told me. "Try to relax. Your grandma's going to be okay. We're going to find her."

I was warming under Diesel's touch. The heat was working its way up my neck and down my spine. It wasn't sexual. It was sensual and soothing. I could feel myself going soft inside. I could feel my heartbeat slowing.

"You have terrific hands," I said to Diesel. "I always get warm when you touch me."

"I've been told it has something to do with sympathetic body chemistry and shared electrical energy. The person who told me that was full of mushrooms, but I thought it sounded cool. The other explanation is that my body temperature runs higher than normal, and I like touching you."

I didn't know I'd fallen asleep until I woke up. I was snuggled against Diesel, and he was watching a basketball game. Snuggy was watching, too. He was in his new clothes, which looked exactly like his old clothes, except the wrinkles and knee bags and ketchup stains were missing. Doug was in the kitchen with the light off. Guess Doug wasn't a Knicks fan.

It was nine o'clock and my mother was probably pacing the floor, waiting for me to bring Grandma home. I tapped her number into my phone and imagined her jumping at the first ring.

"Where are you?"

"I'm home."

"Where's your grandmother?"

"I sort of lost her."

"What?"

"Remember how, in the beginning, she took off on a road trip? It's a little like that. But I don't think she's gone too far this time."

"How could this happen?"

"She's very wily."

"I don't understand. She has a nice home here. Why would she do this?"

"I think she needs to have an adventure once in a while. And she's overly curious."

"You get that from her," my mother said. "You're a lot like your grandmother."

Sort of a scary thought, but I knew it was true. Even at this moment, I had a horse in my kitchen.

"Don't worry," I said to my mother. "She's fine. I'll find her and bring her home tomorrow."

Diesel pulled himself away from the game when I disconnected. "How did that go?"

"As well as could be expected. I would have gotten grounded if she didn't need me to find my grandmother."

"I bet you got grounded a lot when you were a kid."

I laughed out loud, remembering. "I used to climb out the bathroom window."

"Was Morelli waiting for you at the bottom?"

"No. I only had a couple isolated experiences with Morelli back then. He was one of those hit-and-run guys."

"And now?"

"Now he's waiting for me at the bottom." I did some mental knuckle-cracking. "I feel like I should be doing something. I hate sitting here knowing Grandma is locked in Delvina's trunk."

My cell phone rang and for a moment the number displayed didn't register. Then it hit me. Briggs. I'd totally forgotten about him.

"Yes?" I said.

"Where is everybody?"

"We're back in Trenton. Where are you?"

"I'm in Atlantic City. I'm on a roll. I'm shooting craps with my lucky Edna money and I can't lose. Why'd everyone leave?"

"Lou Delvina kidnapped Grandma."

"Get out!"

"I think it's safe to assume you're unemployed."

"Jeez. Did you get her back yet?"

"No. We're working on it. We need a hundred and forty thousand dollars to ransom her. How much have you won?"

"Not that much."

"Keep rolling," I said. And I disconnected.

9

I slapped the alarm button on my bedside clock, but the ringing continued.

"Phone," Diesel murmured against my ear.

I fumbled for the phone and mumbled hello.

"I just got off a triple shift," Morelli said. "Gang fight in the projects. Two dead. Do you want to meet me for breakfast before I crash?"

"What time is it?"

"Six-thirty."

"I've got a full house here. I think I should stay and keep my eye on things."

"Who's there?"

"Diesel and Snuggy O'Connor and Doug."

"Snuggy O'Connor," Morelli said. "I know that name from somewhere."

"He was a jockey. He's here with Doug."

"And Doug is who?"

"Doug's a horse."

There was a long moment of silence.

"They're not all in your apartment, are they?" Morelli asked.

"Yep."

"Is Doug a **little** horse?"

"No. Doug is a big horse. It's complicated."

"It always is," Morelli said. "I'm really tired. Probably I'm hallucinating this whole conversation. I'll call in a day or two when I wake up."

Diesel was in the bed with me, fully clothed except for shoes. I'd also fallen asleep in my clothes . . . minus my bra. The bra was dangling from the doorknob. I didn't want to dwell on how it got there.

"What are you doing in my bed?" I asked Diesel.

"You fell asleep watching television, so I carried you in here and figured you wouldn't mind if I joined you. I don't fit on your couch, and I'm not in love with sleeping on the floor. Did you put in for a wake-up call?"

"That was Morelli coming off a triple shift. Checking in."

I got up and peeked into the living room. No horse. No Snuggy. I went to the bedroom window and pulled the curtain aside. Snuggy and Doug were on a patch of grass at the back of my parking lot. Doug limped when he walked.

"Doug's leg is bothering him," I said to Diesel. "It makes me feel sad to see him limping. I bet he was a sight when he was young and healthy."

"He'll be okay," Diesel said. "We'll find a way to get him healed."

I nodded and blinked to keep from

tearing up. Between Doug and Grandma, I had a lot of painful emotions clogging my throat.

"I'm going to take a shower," I said to Diesel.

"Would you like company?"

"No, but thanks for offering."

"The least I could do," Diesel said.

I got clean clothes, locked myself in the bathroom, and stepped into the shower. When I got out, I felt reenergized.

"I got an idea while you were in the shower," Diesel said. "We need money, right? Who has money sitting around? Delvina. I watched the duffel bag get carried into the car wash, and I didn't see it come out. I'm guessing Delvina has the money in the car wash safe."

"And?"

"And we steal the money from Delvina. Then we can give it back to him to get Grandma. I swear, sometimes I'm so brilliant I can hardly stand it."

"Only problem is, how do we steal the money without getting caught?"

"We need a diversion."

"Oh boy. Been there, done that."

"It's going to have to be a much better diversion. Something clever. Let me jump in the shower and change my clothes and we'll go do some recon."

Snuggy, Diesel, and I sat in my car across from the car wash and watched the action. Friday was senior citizen discount day, and at eight o'clock, business was already jumping.

"This is going to be tough," I said to Diesel. "Too many people. We should have done this last night, when it was dark."

"I didn't think of it last night. Let's get out and walk around. Get a different perspective. See if we can come up with an angle."

Diesel crossed the street, walked half a

block down, and then doubled back, coming up behind the building. Snuggy and I walked in the opposite direction on the other side of the street.

A Doberman was sitting in a small front yard, watching traffic. He was wearing a collar with a little box attached.

"Invisible fence," Snuggy said. "There's a wire buried under the ground, and he gets zapped if he crosses it." He smiled at the dog. "How's it going?"

The dog looked at Snuggy.

"Wow, no kidding," Snuggy said.

"What?" I asked.

"He says he ate a sock, and he's waiting to crap it out. That's why he's outside. Ordinarily, he's inside at this time of the day."

The Doberman stood, concentrated for a moment, and sat back down. Guess the sock wasn't ready to leave.

"We're doing surveillance," Snuggy said to the dog. "I'm a leprechaun and the guy who owns the car wash has my lucky money locked up in his safe."

The dog's eyes widened ever so slightly. Either he was impressed with the leprechaun thing or else the sock was moving south.

"Swear to God," Snuggy said. "I'd just pop over there and take it, but I'm having trouble with my leprechaun invisibility."

The Doberman looked Snuggy up and down.

"Really? Are you sure?" Snuggy said.

"Tell me," I said. "What? **What?**"

Snuggy thunked the heel of his hand against his forehead. "Of course. Why didn't I think of that? It's so obvious."

"What's obvious? What didn't you think of?"

"No time to explain, but I know what went wrong. Tell Diesel not to worry. I'll take care of everything. You guys get in the car and pick me up when I come out of the office."

"Wait! We should discuss this. What did the dog say to you?"

"He said it was my clothes! You see, it all makes sense. I was invisible, but my clothes weren't. It was probably the new laundry detergent I used. All I have to do is take my clothes off, and then I can go in and open the safe and take the money, and no one will see me."

"No, no, no, no. Bad idea."

Snuggy shrugged out of his jacket and shirt and kicked his shoes off. I frantically waved at Diesel, but he was making his way around the building and didn't see me. I made a grab for Snuggy and missed.

"Trust me. This will work," Snuggy said, dancing away, unzipping his green pants.

Snuggy had tighty whities under the green pants, and in an instant, they were on the ground and Snuggy was running across the street.

"Eeek!" I said. And I clapped my hands over my eyes. When I took my hands away, I saw Snuggy's lily-white leprechaun ass hop the curb and sprint for the car wash office door.

The office door opened and a big Sasquatch-type uniformed car wash guy looked out at Snuggy. "What the fuck?"

Diesel was on the sidewalk, rooted to the spot. He looked at Snuggy in amazement and then he looked across the street at me.

I shrugged and made an **I don't know, but it's not my fault** gesture.

Snuggy danced around in front of the car wash guy. "'Tis invisible I be, and lucky fer you or t'wud be the wrath o' me shillelagh ye'd be feelin'."

"Your shillelagh don't look like anything to worry about," the guy said.

A couple more uniformed guys stopped work and looked over at Snuggy.

"What's with him?" one of them said.

"He thinks he's a leprechaun," Sasquatch told him.

"No way," the guy said. "Leprechauns got red hair down there."

Everyone stared at Snuggy's thatch and exposed plumbing, including Snuggy.

"Cripes, I've smoked fatter joints than that," one of the guys said. "I didn't know they came that small."

"I'm supposed to be invisible," Snuggy said.

Several cars were lined up to take advantage of senior discount day. The drivers honked their horns at Snuggy and yelled at him out of their windows.

"You're holding up the line."

"Get out of the way. You think I have all day to do this?"

"Pervert!"

"Somebody shoot him."

"You should come nice and peaceful with us," Sasquatch said. "We'll take you to the hospital. They got a special room set aside for leprechauns."

Sasquatch reached for Snuggy, and Snuggy yelped and jumped away. The men ran after Snuggy, and Snuggy took off in blind panic, running around the cars that were waiting in line. Two more uniformed car wash attendants joined the chase, and the sheer number of people running after Snuggy added to his confusion. The seniors kept honking their horns and everyone was yelling.

"Catch him!"

"Cut him off on the other side."

"Go left."

"Go right."

It probably only took a couple minutes, but it seemed like it went on for hours, with Snuggy shrieking like a girl, waving his arms in the air as he ran. He dodged two guys, sprinted straight into the car wash tunnel, and disappeared from view behind a curtain of water.

"Eeeeeeeyiiii!" Snuggy squealed inside the tunnel.

The car wash guys ran in after Snuggy, but Snuggy was the only one who ran out. He was soaking wet and clumped with soapsuds, and he was moving at light speed. Sasquatch crawled out on his hands and knees, and two more men windmilled out and fell on their asses in the soapy water.

Diesel came from out of nowhere, grabbed the back of my sweatshirt, and yanked me toward the car. "Get in!" Diesel yelled at me.

I jumped in next to Diesel, and he rocketed away from the curb. Snuggy was running down the street in front of us, knees high, arms pumping, not looking back. Diesel honked the horn at him and pulled alongside. Snuggy ripped the back door open and threw himself in.

"Damn Doberman," Snuggy said. "I

should have known better than to trust a Doberman. They're all practical jokers."

I was facing forward, not wanting to look at Snuggy naked in my backseat. Snuggy naked wasn't an inspiring sight.

"You've had this happen before with a Doberman?" I asked him.

"I never learn," Snuggy said. "I'm too trusting. Are these my clothes?"

"Yeah. I picked them up off the ground and put them in the car. I figured sooner or later you'd get cold."

"Thanks," Snuggy said. "That was real nice of you."

I looked down at my feet and realized that I was sharing space with the duffel bag. "How'd this get here?"

"No one was paying attention to the office," Diesel said. "Everyone was chasing Snuggy. So I scrambled the security system, walked in, opened the safe, and took the money."

I opened the bag and counted the money. It was all there. "Woohoo! Did anyone see you?"

"No. I went in and out through a back door. The office was empty."

Snuggy was dressed by the time we got back to my apartment. He still had some suds in his hair, but aside from that, he looked okay. I opened the door to my apartment, and Doug was stomping around in my kitchen.

"Doug has to go," Snuggy said.

"Go where?"

"Out! Hold the elevator."

I ran to the elevator and punched the button. The doors opened, Snuggy and Doug trotted down the hall, and we got into the elevator. Doug was dancing around, looking frantic. He lifted his tail, there was the sound of air escaping from a balloon, and the elevator filled with horse fart.

"Holy crap!" I said.

"Doug says he's sorry. He says it slipped out."

The doors opened, and we all rushed into the lobby and out into the parking lot. Doug took a wide stance and whizzed for about fifteen minutes. He walked around a little and dropped a load of road apples. We had a pooper-scooper law in Trenton, but I wasn't sure it applied to horse shit. I'd need a snow shovel and a twenty-gallon garbage bag to pooper-scooper what Doug dropped.

"Maybe an apartment isn't the best place for Doug," I said to Snuggy.

"He's too cramped in the RV. I don't know where else to put him."

"I have a friend who owns a building with a parking garage. It's very secure and the garage is well lit and really clean." Actually, cleaner than my apartment.

"That might be okay," Snuggy said. "He'd have room to walk around in a parking garage. And maybe I could bring some straw in for him to stand on just for a couple days until his surgery."

I dialed Ranger.

"Yo," Ranger said.

"Yo yourself. I was wondering if I could park something in your garage for a couple days."

"Something?"

"A horse."

A moment of silence.

"Babe," Ranger said.

"He used to be a racehorse."

More silence.

"He's sort of a homeless horse," I said.

"I'm leaving for the airport in two seconds, and I won't be back for a couple days. You can put the horse in the garage, but I don't want that horse in my apartment."

"Who would put a horse in an apartment? That's dumb."

"Where's the horse staying now?"

"My apartment."

"I can always count on you to brighten my day," Ranger said. And he disconnected.

I ran upstairs to tell Diesel and to get my purse.

"Snuggy can stay with Doug as long as he promises not to leave Rangeman property," Diesel said.

"I'm going to ride over with Snuggy. I'll be back as soon as I get them settled in. I thought I'd call Delvina before I go."

Diesel was foraging in the refrigerator. He found the leftover pizza and dug in. "If he lets you choose the exchange site, ask for the car wash again."

I called Delvina and told him we had the money.

"I'll get back to you," Delvina said. "I gotta make arrangements."

"The car wash was good last time," I told him. "Why don't we do the car wash again?"

"The car wash won't work for this," Delvina said. "I'll find someplace better and call you back."

We had enough overhead clearance to drive the RV into the underground Rangeman garage. We parked to one side and we off-loaded Doug.

The elevator doors opened and Hal stepped out. Hal was Rangeman muscle, with a body like a stegosaurus. He was dressed in Rangeman black, his blond hair had been freshly buzzed, and his face was brightened by a smile.

"This is a horse," Hal said, looking like an eight-year-old on Christmas morning.

"Ranger told me I could park him here for a couple days."

The smile got wider. "He's big."

"He was a racehorse."

"No kidding? Wow. I'm supposed to get you whatever you need."

"A couple bales of straw would be perfect," Snuggy said.

"Sure. And we have a bay over on the other side where we wash the cars. You can get water there. Just give me a holler if you need anything else."

"I could use a ride home," I said to Hal. "I'm going to leave the RV here."

Snuggy and I hauled Doug's food and buckets out of the RV, and Snuggy looked at the hose on the far wall.

"I'd like to clean up the sore on Doug's leg and rewrap it with a fresh bandage," Snuggy said. "I found some gauze bandages in the bathroom, but there's not enough soap."

I had a gizmo on my keychain that got me into the Rangeman garage and Ranger's private apartment. I rode the elevator to the seventh floor, let myself into Ranger's lair, and went straight to his bathroom. I grabbed a bottle of shower gel and returned to the garage. It was Ranger's Bulgari Green, and I'd probably get a rush every time I smelled Doug, but it was the fastest solution.

"I have to go," I said to Snuggy. "If there's a problem, you can call Hal or me. I'll have someone drop food and clean clothes off for you. Diesel says you're not to leave the Rangeman building."

I parked the RV against the wall, and Hal pulled alongside in a black Explorer. We drove past the car wash on the way to my apartment. It was all business as usual. No one was running around looking like a robbery had just been committed. Fingers crossed that they wouldn't open the safe and freak. I didn't want anything to go wrong. I was excited about getting my hands on Grandma.

I thanked Hal and hurried into the lobby. Dillon Ruddick, the building super, and a couple tenants were milling around in front of the open elevator.

"I've never smelled anything like it," Mrs. Ruiz said. "I got out of the elevator, and it wouldn't go away. It's stuck in my clothes."

"It's a horse fart," Mr. Klein said. "There's manure in the parking lot, and the elevator smells like a horse fart. Some- one's keeping a horse in this building."

"That's ridiculous," Mrs. Ruiz said. "Who would do such a thing?"

Everyone turned and looked at me.

"Do you smell it?" Mr. Klein asked.

"What?"

"Horse fart."

"I thought that was the guy in 3C."

Dillon snorted and grinned at me. Not a lot got by Dillon, but he was a good guy, and you could buy him with a six-pack. I ducked into the stairs and ran up a flight.

Diesel was at the dining room table, working at my computer. "Delvina called," Diesel said. "He wanted to make the exchange in an abandoned factory at

the end of Stark Street. I told him that
didn't work for us. He won't do it at the
car wash again. I don't think he knows the
money is missing, but he's uncomfortable.
He's kidnapped an old lady. That's different from a horse. That's a trip to the big
house."

"Did you settle on a location?"

"I wanted it someplace public. He
wanted it someplace isolated. He's afraid
the police are involved. It's a reasonable
fear. We agreed to meet in the multiplex
parking lot."

"Which multiplex?"

"Hamilton Township."

"That theater went bankrupt. It's
boarded up."

"Yeah, I would have preferred to have
more people around. I'm going to make
the exchange. I don't trust Delvina. He's
too nervous. I want you on the roof with
a rifle."

"I'm not actually a gun person. If you

want a sharpshooter, that would be Connie."

"Then get Connie. The exchange is set to take place at noon. I need to have you and Connie on the roof at least an hour ahead. The front of the parking lot is wide open. The back is up against an alley that gives access to the Dumpsters. To the other side of the alley is a greenbelt. So you should be able to sneak in the back door and get up on the roof. I'll make sure all the doors are open for you. I've been pulling up aerial shots of the area on your computer, and I think this will work."

10

"We have the money to ransom Grandma," I told Connie and Lula when I got to the bonds office. "The exchange is going to take place at noon in the parking lot of the bankrupt multiplex in Hamilton Township."

"Where'd you get that kind of money?" Lula asked.

"Diesel picked it up."

"He's the man," Lula said.

"He needs a sharpshooter on the roof, covering his back," I said to Connie. "Can you take a couple hours off today?"

"Sure," Connie said. "I'll pick out something nice from the back room."

The back room to the bonds office contained a mess of confiscated items ranging from toaster ovens to Harleys to computers and televisions. It also housed an arsenal. Connie had a crate of handcuffs bought at a fire sale, boxes of ammunition for just about every gun in the universe, handguns, shotguns, rifles, machine guns, knives, a couple tasers, and a rocket launcher.

"I'm not exactly chopped liver with a gun," Lula said. "I'll come, too."

Lula was only a marginally better shot than me. The difference between Lula and me was that Lula was willing to shoot at most anything.

A half hour later, Lula parked her Firebird on the far side of the greenbelt, and we bushwhacked our way through the vegetation to the alley. The alley was empty and the back door to the theater was unlocked. Connie had a sniper rifle equipped with a high-powered scope and laser, plus a purse filled with assorted toys. Lula had chosen an assault rifle. And I was elected to carry the ammo and the rocket launcher.

"I really don't think we need a rocket launcher," I said to Lula.

"Better safe than sorry," Lula said. "And anyways, I always wanted to fire off one of them rockets."

Connie went in first, and we all followed the beam from her flashlight through the dark theater and up the fire stairs to the door that led to the roof. The door was unlocked, as promised. The roof was flat and tarred. The sun was weak in a gray sky, heavy with clouds and the threat of rain. I was wearing a sweatshirt under a windbreaker, and I felt the chill creeping through the layers.

I could see why Diesel had chosen this particular building. We were able to hide behind an elaborate stucco false front and still see everything in the lot below. Lula and Connie found positions they liked. I found a place where I could see the action and not get in the way.

"I feel just like a SWAT guy," Lula said. "If I'd known, I'd have dressed appropriately."

As it was, Lula was in four-inch stilettos, a short black spandex skirt that almost fit her, an orange spandex T-shirt, and a matching orange faux fur jacket.

We hunkered in to wait for the exchange, and at eleven-thirty, we heard a car pull up to the back of the building. We ran to the back and looked down at a black Lincoln Town Car. Two men got out and tried the door. We'd locked the door after we'd entered, so they went to the trunk of the Town Car, got a tire iron, beat the crap out of the door, and pried it open. They went back to the trunk, got a couple rifles, and disappeared into the building.

"I bet they're Delvina guys," Lula said. "They're probably coming up to the roof."

Connie nodded in agreement.

"Well, tough tooties," Lula said. "We were here first. We got dibs on the roof."

"I think we need to ice them," Connie said. "Anybody bring cuffs?"

"I got some," Lula said. She stuck her head in her purse and, after some rooting around, came up with two pair.

Connie and Lula stood on either side of the door and waited for the men. The door opened, the men appeared, and Connie raised her rifle.

"Freeze," Connie said. "Drop your weapons. Hands in the air."

They both turned and looked at her.

"What the fuck?" the one guy said.

They were middle-aged thugs, dressed in bowling shirts and Sansabelt slacks. Their hair was slicked back. Their shoes were scuffed and run down at the heel. Their guns weren't as big as ours.

"Guns on the ground," Connie said.

"And what if we don't do that? You girls gonna get tough?"

Connie shot a hole in his foot. Actually, it was mostly just a chunk taken off the side of his shoe, but from the way he dropped his gun and started jumping around, you could assume she'd nicked his little toe.

"Fuck, fuck, fuck," he yelled. "What the fuck!"

There were a bunch of pipes running along the roof that attached to air-conditioning units. Lula patted both men down and cuffed them to one of the pipes.

"What about my foot?" the one guy asked. "Look at it. It's bleeding. I need a doctor."

"If either of you makes a single sound, I'm going to shoot you in the other foot," Connie said.

We went back to our positions in the front of the building and watched the lot.

At exactly noon, two cars slowly drove into view. One was a black Town Car. The other was my Monte Carlo. The cars parked a good distance apart and sat at idle. The driver's side door to the Town Car opened and Mickey got out. Diesel got out of the Monte and ambled over. Surfer dude meets the Mob.

They stood talking for a moment, Diesel with his hands loose at his sides and a black canvas messenger bag hung on his shoulder. Diesel handed the messenger bag to Mickey. Mickey turned to leave, and Diesel wrapped his hand around the bag's shoulder strap.

"Not so fast. I want Grandma."

His voice was soft, but it carried up to us.

"Sure," Mickey said. "She's in the car. I'll go get her."

"I'll keep the bag until you come back," Diesel said.

Mickey shook his finger at him. "You have trust issues."

"People keep telling me that."

Mickey walked to the car and opened the back door. Grandma lurched out, gave Mickey the finger, and harrumphed over to Diesel. Diesel passed the messenger bag to Mickey and took possession of Grandma.

I almost collapsed with relief. I had to hold on to the wall to keep from sinking to my knees.

"Hold on," Lula said. "There's another car coming."

It was black, and it was moving fast. Diesel glanced at the car, grabbed Grandma's hand, and pulled her toward the Monte Carlo. The black car slid to a stop in front of the Monte and four men jumped out with guns drawn. Diesel changed direction and ran to the movie entrance with Grandma.

One of the men took aim, Connie picked him off, and everyone looked up to the roof. A second guy fired two shots at us, and Lula let loose with the assault rifle. It was like **war**. The three remaining men ducked behind their car and returned Lula's fire. Mickey and Delvina were out and shooting. And Diesel and Grandma scooted into the theater.

"This is bullshit," Lula said. "This here's the United States. We don't go around blasting the shit out of people here. Well, okay, maybe in the projects, but hell, this here's the friggin' multiplex. There's things you don't do in the multiplex. Gimme that rocket launcher. I'll fix their ass."

"Do you know how to work it?" I asked.

"What's to know? It's point and shoot, right? They give these suckers to pinheads who join the army. How hard could it be? Just prop this big boy up for me, and I'll do the rest."

I covered my ears and closed my eyes and **phuunf!** The bird was away. We all looked over the edge of the building and **BANG.** The rocket blew up my car.

"Must be something wrong with the sight," Lula said. "At least you don't have to drive a car that's got no reverse."

The Monte was a fireball.

"You got insurance, right?" Lula asked.

Delvina and his men stood in open-mouthed shock for a beat. Then they all dove into their cars and drove away. Diesel opened the door and looked out at my car. He was hands on hips, and from my perch high above him, I could see he was smiling. You want to make a man smile . . . just blow up a car with a rocket.

Rain had started misting down on us. I packed up the ammo, and Lula and Connie shouldered their rifles.

"Hey," the guy with the shot-off toe said. "What about us?"

"Someone will come up here looking for you . . . probably," Connie said.

"Yeah, but it's raining. I'm gonna get a cold."

"Hold on," Lula said, peering over the edge of the building. "The one black car is coming back."

Connie and I ran to the edge and looked down. It was Delvina's car. It pulled up to the front door, and Delvina got out and stormed into the building.

"You guys stay here and make sure no one else goes in," I said. "I'm going downstairs to help Diesel."

"Here," Connie said. "Take my flashlight and this microwave stunner. It's new. Vinnie won it in a crap game last week. Just point it like a gun and pull the trigger. It doesn't do any permanent damage, but it makes your skin feel like it's on fire."

I took the stunner and ran down the stairs into the dark lobby. I stood and listened. There was a corridor to my left and a corridor to my right. Multiple movie theaters opened off the two corridors. I thought I heard movement in the right corridor. I crept along, hand to the wall, feeling my way in total blackness. I didn't want to give myself away by using the flashlight.

I stopped and listened again. I was at the entrance to one of the theaters, and I could hear the very faint murmur of voices. I held my breath and eased inside. I tiptoed up the ramp that led to the stadium seating and cautiously moved into the aisle.

Delvina, Diesel, and Grandma were about twenty rows in front of me. Grandma and Diesel were facing me, caught in the glare of Delvina's flashlight. I saw Diesel's eyes flick to me for a nanosecond and return to Delvina.

"You know how I found you in here?" Delvina said to Grandma and Diesel. "I got a nose for it. I didn't get where I am for no reason. I'm cagey. And I got a nose for danger. I see danger and I get rid of it. You know what I'm saying?"

"No," Grandma said. "You're a nut."

"I'm saying you're disturbing my comfort level," Delvina said. "So I'm gonna have to get rid of you. Both of you. I should have gotten rid of you last month when you gave me this rash," he said to Diesel. "I know it was you. And you said you were gonna turn me into a toad, and now look at me. It's happening."

I aimed the stunner at Delvina's neck and hit the GO button.

"Yow," Delvina said, slapping at his neck.

He still had the gun trained on Grandma, but he was hopping around, and I couldn't keep the microwave stunner on target.

"It's you," he said to Diesel. "You're sending bugs to bite me, right? Fire bugs. I know you're not normal. O'Connor even said so. He said you had these **skills**. You and that horse. You're in this together, aren't you? Putting thoughts in my head."

"What kind of thoughts?" Grandma wanted to know.

"Horse thoughts," Delvina said. "He talks to me. I hear him in my head. What kind of horse does that?"

"Maybe he's an alien horse," Grandma said. "I saw a television show once about how these aliens came down to this place in Arizona and were controlling people's minds and making them go on all these porno sites on the Internet."

Delvina stopped moving, and I aimed for the hand that was holding the gun. He yelped, dropped the gun, and grabbed his hand.

"Get him!" Grandma yelled.

Delvina grabbed her, shoved her into Diesel, and took off running. By the time Diesel had untangled himself from Grandma, Delvina was out of the theater. I ran after him, but he had a good head start. Surprising how fast he could move his bloated body on his skinny little toad legs.

I heard shots being fired from the roof and it sounded like shots were being returned from the theater entrance. I flicked the flashlight off so I wouldn't be an easy target, and I came to a dead stop in the dark. Diesel came up behind me, grabbed my hand, and pulled me along, the two of us running flat-out. Me in blind trust, and Diesel not having a problem seeing.

We turned into the lobby, partially lit from the glass entrance doors, and beyond the glass doors I saw the black car take off.

Diesel and I pushed through the doors and stood against the building, sheltered from the rain, and watched the black car race out of the lot. My Monte Carlo was burning out of control in front of us.

"This is a pip of a fire," Grandma said, coming up behind us with Lula and Connie.

"I was inside the theater, but I saw the Monte Carlo get hit," Diesel said. "Who shot the rocket off?"

"I might have done that," Lula said. "I'm pretty sure that launcher was defective."

"Are you okay?" I asked Grandma.

"I could use some lipstick."

Lula dropped Grandma, Diesel, and me at my apartment. We waved good-bye and walked into the small lobby. The elevator doors were locked into the open position and a fan had been placed inside the elevator. Behind the fan was a pop-up spring meadow air freshener.

"Someone must have left a stinker in there," Grandma said.

We took the stairs and shuffled down the hall. There was a slight scent of horse when we entered my apartment, but it wasn't unpleasant.

"I know this is crazy, but I sort of feel sorry for Lou Delvina," Grandma said. "I heard him talking, and he was saying how his wife left him on account of Diesel giving him the rash and making him all swell up. That's why Delvina wants his money back. So he can buy a big fancy house for his wife. He figures that would get her back." Grandma slid her dentures around a little. "I tell you, that Delvina's only got one oar dipped in the water. It's a real sad thing to see. He used to be a respected mobster. And now he's nutso cuckoo."

I called my mother.

"I have Grandma here in my apartment," I said. "I'll bring her home in a little while."

"Why can't you bring her home now?"

"I'm having car issues."

"I'll send your father for her."

I got Grandma spruced up as best I could, and she was ready to go when my father knocked on my door.

"There's a fat guy who looks like a toad out in your parking lot," my father said. "He's talking to himself, and I think he's making a Molotov cocktail."

We all went to my window and looked out. Lou Delvina was in the lot, standing in the rain, trying to light a rag he'd crammed into a wine bottle. I opened the window and stuck my head out.

"Hey," I said. "What are you doing?"

"I'm doing what I have to do," Delvina yelled up at me.

He lit the rag and heaved the bottle. It crashed through the top pane of my living room window and rolled on the floor. Some of the carpet got singed, but the bottle didn't break. Diesel grabbed the bottle and threw it back out the window. It smashed on the pavement next to Delvina's black Town Car, and the Town Car was almost instantly consumed by flames.

"Eeek!" Delvina shrieked, jumping away from the fire. "Alien voodoo! Someone call the National Guard, Homeland Security, Men in Black." He looked up at Diesel and shook his fist. "You're not gonna get me. I know how it is with you aliens. I know what you do to people. This is a fight to the finish." And Delvina ran out of the lot and disappeared from view.

"Poor man," Grandma said. "Where do you suppose he got the idea Diesel is an alien?"

"As far as I'm concerned, none of this happened," my father said to me. "I didn't see anything. That's what I'm telling your mother."

I closed and locked the door when my father and grandmother left. Fire trucks screamed in the distance and black smoke billowed from the burning car. Diesel taped a plastic garbage bag to the broken window to keep the smoke and rain out of the apartment.

My phone rang and I saw from the display that it was Morelli.

"I hear there's a car burning in your parking lot," Morelli said.

"It's not mine. My car was blown up and burned at the multiplex."

Morelli absorbed this for a beat. "There was a time when I'd freak over that, but now it seems sort of normal. The car in your lot . . . did you set it on fire?"

"Nope."

"Do I need to know any gory details?"

"No. Everything's under control. Diesel taped a garbage bag over the broken window, and the firebomb only singed the carpet a little."

"Great," Morelli said. And he disconnected.

"He take that okay?" Diesel asked.

"I could hear him chewing Rolaids."

11

The smoke stopped rolling past my windows and the unintelligible chatter and squawk of the police band was intermittent. One fire truck and one squad car remained. A tow truck was standing by to haul the remains of Delvina's car off to the auto graveyard. Most of my neighbors were back in their apartments, finding television to be more entertaining than the dismal charred carcass left in the lot.

Diesel and I were in the kitchen eating peanut butter sandwiches. Diesel stopped with a sandwich in hand and listened. "Now what?" he said. He went to the door, and the doorbell rang.

Diesel opened the door to Mickey.

"This is awkward," Mickey said.

Diesel and I looked past Mickey, down the hall.

Mickey shook the rain off his umbrella and propped it up against the wall. "I'm alone. Can I come in?"

"Do you have a bomb?" I asked.

"No. What I got is a headache."

"What's up?"

"I'm looking for Mr. Delvina, and I couldn't help noticing you have a freshly cooked car in your lot that might be the same size as Mr. Delvina's car."

I spread peanut butter on a slice of bread and added some potato chips and olives. "It is, in fact, Mr. Delvina's car," I told Mickey.

"Was Mr. Delvina in it when it got cooked?"

"Unfortunately, no."

"Mr. Delvina isn't a well man," Mickey said.

"No kidding."

"He isn't himself these days. Between you and me, he doesn't have a rash no more, but he likes the medicine. He's been taking more and more of it, and I think it's making him funny in the head."

I finished constructing the sandwich and offered it to Mickey.

"Thank you. I didn't get no lunch. Mr. Delvina was anxious to get to the multiplex. He needs the money to get the missus back, but personally I think he's spending the money on his medicine. Now he's got this idea that Diesel is an alien. It's crazy. It's just crazy."

Mickey took a bite of the sandwich and chewed. "This is delicious," he said. "I don't usually like peanut butter, but this sandwich got everything in it."

"You don't think Diesel is an alien?"

"Of course not. Everyone knows aliens don't look like that. Aliens got them big heads with the big eyes and skinny bodies. They look like what's-his-name . . . Gumby."

"There you have it," I said to Diesel. "You don't look like an alien."

"Good to know," Diesel said.

"Anyways, after Mr. Delvina went goofy at the multiplex, we had a difference of opinion, and he kicked me out of the car and drove away. Mr. Delvina wanted to firebomb this apartment because he thinks you two are doing knicky-knacky here and trying to breed the spawn of the alien devil." Mickey stopped eating and thought about that for a moment. "How did Mr. Delvina's car get cooked?" he asked.

"Firebomb," I told him.

Mickey shook his head. "He never could get the hang of a good firebomb. I always had to make them. It's important to use the right kind of bottle. People think just anyone can make a firebomb, but that isn't so."

"It's a skill," Diesel said.

"Exactly," Mickey said. "We all got special skills, right? Like the boss. He used to be real good at sizing up people. He had instincts." Mickey gave his head a shake. "I feel bad that the boss is wacko. I think I've been one of them enablers. I've been going out and getting him the medicine. I shouldn't have been doing that." Mickey washed his sandwich down with a diet soda. "You should be careful. Mr. Delvina don't give up on something once he gets an idea in his head. Even now that he's screwy." Mickey wrote his phone number on a piece of paper and gave it to me. "Call me if you see Mr. Delvina, and I'll come try to catch him."

Diesel closed the door after Mickey and grinned at me. "People think we're doing knicky-knacky up here."

"Don't get any ideas."

"Too late. I have lots of ideas."

"Are any of them about Lou Delvina?"

"Not right now," Diesel said.

"Delvina's not going to be happy when he opens his safe to deposit the money he got today."

Diesel screwed the top onto the peanut butter jar and put his knife in the dish-washer. "I hate to say this, but we're going to have to find Delvina and neutralize him somehow before he figures out how to build a better bomb."

"Neutralize," I said. "That's very civilized."

"Yeah, I'd feel like a real tough guy if I said I was going to **whack** Delvina, but it wouldn't be true. I'm not a killer."

I went to the window and looked out. The fire truck and police car were gone. Delvina's car was slowly being towed away on a flatbed. Probably there was a cop somewhere in the building going door to door asking questions. I thought it best if we left before he got to the second floor.

I zipped an all-weather jacket over my sweatshirt and hung my purse on my shoulder. "Delvina is on foot. He can steal a car, call a friend, or he can walk to the car wash. I'm betting on the car wash."

We locked the apartment and took the stairs to the lobby. We pushed through the lobby doors and stopped. We didn't have a car.

"Crap," I said. "No car."

Diesel surveyed the cars in the lot. "Pick one."

"You don't kill people, but you steal cars?"

"Yep."

I hauled my cell phone out and I called Lula. "I need a ride to my parents' house."

My father was out running errands and my mother and grandmother were in the kitchen yelling at each other.

"You're grounded," my mother said to my grandmother. "You are not to leave this house."

"Blow it out your ear," my grandmother said.

My mother looked at me when I walked in. "What am I supposed to do with her?"

"I think you should make a deal."

"What kind of deal?"

"How about you buy her a television for her room if she promises not to go off like that ever again."

"I like that deal," Grandma said. "I could use a television in my room. I could watch whatever I wanted if I had my own television."

Everyone has a price.

"I guess that would be okay," my mother said. "We could get you a little flat screen that would sit on your bureau."

"I'm having car problems," I said. "I was wondering if I could borrow Uncle Sandor's Buick."

"Sure," my grandmother said. "Help yourself."

When my Great-Uncle Sandor went into the nursing home, he left his 1953 powder-blue-and-white Buick to Grandma Mazur. Grandma Leadfoot had her license revoked and isn't able to drive the car, but the car lives in my father's garage for emergency use.

"Sweet Thing, you've got a heck of a gene pool," Diesel said, following me out of the house. "Your grandmother is fearless. She's not even afraid of your mother."

"Grandma's philosophy is **now or never**."

I opened the garage door and Diesel's smile widened. "This is a **car**."

Actually, it only looked like a car. It drove like a refrigerator on wheels. I gave Diesel the keys and climbed onto the passenger seat.

Diesel powered the car out of the Burg to Hamilton Avenue, and we cruised by the car wash. Not a lot going on in the rain. No sign of Delvina. We'd watched for him on the way over with Lula and hadn't seen him then, either.

"What will we do if we find Delvina?" I asked Diesel.

"Good question. If he was a normal person, we could sit on him and get him detoxed. Unfortunately, I don't think detoxing Delvina will entirely eliminate his desire to kill us."

We parked across the street half a block away, and I called Connie. "Tell me about Delvina's car wash. What does he do with it? Launder money? Run numbers? Pimp out hookers?"

"All of the above," Connie said. "I'm not sure about the laundering, but it's a cash operation, so it stands to reason he washes more than cars."

"How about employees? Would anyone have access to the safe besides Delvina?"

"So far as I know, he hires a bunch of dumb kids. If anyone else had access to the safe, I'd think it was his stooge, Mickey."

"Okay, here's what we've got," I said to Diesel. "He kidnapped Grandma and extorted Snuggy. He runs numbers out of the car wash, has a stable of hookers, and probably washes money. Surely we can get him sent away for at least one of those."

We'd sat there for a half hour and I was getting twitchy. Time was passing and Delvina was out there plotting God-knew-what.

My cell phone rang and I snatched it out of my purse.

"Delvina was here," Connie said. "He burst into the office like a crazy person, ranting and waving a gun around. He said he was looking for you and the alien. I'm guessing that would be Diesel. Clearly, neither of you was here, so he took off. He was rambling on about how you vacated your apartment, but he'd track you down. I think he might be going to your parents' house next. He said he knew where you lived."

"Stay here in the Buick and watch the car wash," Diesel said. "I'll go to your parents' house. If Delvina shows up, don't make a move. Just sit tight and call me."

"Take the Buick. It'll be faster."

He was out of the car. "I don't need the Buick."

"You aren't going to steal a car, are you?"

"Close your eyes and count to a hundred."

I closed my eyes and counted to twenty. I opened my eyes and Diesel was gone. I looked down the street. Was a car missing from the curb?

The rain had dropped back to a drizzle. It streaked the windshield and shimmered on the street. It was midafternoon and traffic was picking up. A black Town Car pulled into the car wash lot and parked behind the office. The rear quarter panel of the car was peppered with bullet holes. The headlights blinked off, and Mickey got out of the car and went into the office through the back door.

Minutes later, an armored truck rolled down the street, pulled into the lot, and parked beside the Town Car. Delvina got out of the armored truck and walked to the building, carrying the messenger bag. He was wearing a bulky raincoat, and his head was wrapped in aluminum foil.

I tapped Diesel's number into my cell phone and the number instantly went to voicemail. "Delvina's here," I said and disconnected.

I sat for a couple moments and ran out of patience. I got out of the car and ran across the street to the car wash. I crept around the building, hoping to see in a window, but had no luck. I very slowly and silently turned the knob to the back door and eased the door open just a crack.

The office was basically one large room with a front door opening into the car wash lobby and a back door opening to the parking lot. I peeked through the crack and saw Delvina and Mickey in front of the safe.

"You got a what?" Mickey asked.

"An armored car. I'm taking my money and I'm going to Kansas. I read where it's safer from aliens in the middle of the country."

"That's crazy. And what about the missus and her new house?"

"Screw the missus. I don't even want a new house. I don't know what was wrong with the old house. Anyway, this is serious. I'm gonna get rid of this alien, but there might be more. They travel in packs or pods or something." Delvina took a bottle out of his pocket and popped some pills into his mouth.

"You should go easy on those pills," Mickey said. "I think they might be making you goofy."

"I need these pills. I got a rash."

"I don't see no rash."

"That's because I'm taking the pills, stupid."

"What are you wearing on your head? Is that for the rain?"

"It's so they can't control my mind. You know how we use aluminum foil to scramble the GPS when we hijack a truck? It's the same with aliens. You wear this aluminum foil on your head, and they can't fuck with your mind."

"I guess that makes sense, but I'm not convinced they're aliens. They don't look like aliens."

"That's because they're shape-shifters. Remember when we used to watch **Star Trek**?"

"Yeah, them shape-shifters were nasty buggers."

"Anyway, I'm sorry I kicked you out of the car, and I didn't mean it when I fired you," Delvina said. "It's just you weren't making any sense."

"Maybe, but I don't see where we want to make trouble with that big guy Diesel and the Plum woman."

"It's us or them," Delvina said. "Anybody can see that."

Delvina set the black canvas messenger bag on the floor by the safe and spun the dial. He fed in the combination, pulled the door open, and gasped. No duffel bag in the safe.

"Where's the bag?" he asked Mickey. "Where's the money?"

"It's in the safe," Mickey said.

"The safe's friggin' empty."

"That's impossible. Only you and me's got the combination. How would the safe get empty? Maybe you took the money out and forgot."

Color was oozing into Delvina's face. "I got a mind like a steel trap. I don't forget nothing. I'm no dummy."

"Yeah, but boss, you been taking a lot of pills lately."

"Stop with the pills. I know what I'm doing. You're the one who don't know what he's doing." Delvina tapped his finger against the aluminum foil. "You're not protecting your brain like I am. And I'm smart enough to know who took the money."

"Who took it?" Mickey asked.

"You took it," Delvina said.

"I don't think so. I don't remember taking it."

"You took it because I fired you. Thought you'd get away with it."

"That's insulting. I wouldn't do something like that."

"I want my money," Delvina yelled at Mickey. "Give it to me."

"I don't got it. I swear."

Delvina grabbed a double-barreled shotgun from a gun rack on the wall. "This is your last chance."

Mickey's eyes looked like they were about to pop out of their sockets. "That's nuts."

Delvina raised the shotgun and Mickey took off for the back door. I jumped away and Mickey ran out of the building, slamming the door shut behind him. **BAM!** Delvina blasted a cantaloupe-size hole in the door. Mickey threw himself into the Town Car and cranked it over.

I looked down at my feet and told them to run, but they didn't do anything.

Delvina kicked the door open and aimed at the car, but the car was already skidding out of the lot. I was standing behind the door and would have been hidden except for the big hole in it.

"You!" Delvina said. And he turned the shotgun on me.

I was total deer in the headlights. I was openmouthed, heart-thumping frozen.

"Get in the office," he said. "Go!"

I stumbled inside and tried to pull it together. I didn't think he'd shoot me if I didn't make any sudden moves. Diesel was the guy he really wanted. He'd use me to get Diesel.

Delvina took cuffs out of the top desk drawer. He dropped them on the desk and took a step back with the shotgun still trained on me. "Put them on."

I cuffed myself with my hands in front. If you're serious about restraining someone, you never do this. Hands are always cuffed behind, but Delvina didn't seem to care.

"Okay," he said. "Where is he?"

My mind was racing. I needed to get Delvina into a position where he'd be at a disadvantage. I was afraid if we stayed in the office, Diesel might walk in and get blown away. I decided my best chance

at survival was to take Delvina to Rangeman and have Ranger's crew come to my
rescue.

"Diesel went to check on Snuggy and
Doug," I said. "They're hidden in a parking garage downtown."

"Then that's where we're going." He
motioned to the door with the shotgun.
"Walk."

I squinted into the misting rain when
I stepped outside. I didn't see Diesel. I
didn't see Mickey returning with an atten-
dant from the psychiatric ward at St.
Francis. What I saw was an armored
truck.

"Get in," Delvina said. "You're driving."

"That might not be a good idea," I said.
"I've never driven an armored truck
before."

"It's like any other truck. It's even auto-
matic. Just get in before I shoot you. It's

raining on my aluminum foil. It's real loud in my head. Like rain on a tin roof."

I hauled myself up onto the driver's seat and put my cuffed hands on the wheel. "You're going to have to turn the key and put it into reverse," I told Delvina.

I inched my way back, Delvina put it into drive, and I inched my way out of the lot. I had no rear visibility except for the side mirrors. Narrow bulletproof windshield. My hands were cuffed together, and the monster drove like a freight train. I was afraid I'd run over a Dodge Neon and never know.

"Where did you get this?" I asked Delvina.

"Borrowed it."

Oh boy.

I rolled over a couple curbs and took out a mailbox, but I kept going.

"Cripes," Delvina said. "You're the worst driver I've ever seen."

Obviously, he'd never driven with Grandma. Considering I couldn't see for shit and my hands were cuffed, I thought I was doing an okay job. I didn't mow down the crossing guard, and I'd stopped for most of the lights.

"Where are we going?" Delvina wanted to know.

"It's on the next block. It's the narrow building with the underground garage."

I crept down the street and eased the nose of the armored truck up to the garage security gate.

"Now what?" Delvina asked.

Now I was supposed to flash my key card, but my key card was in my purse and my purse was in the Buick.

"I forgot about the security gate," I said.

Delvina put the truck in reverse. "Back it up a couple feet."

I slowly moved the truck back.

Delvina put the truck in drive. "Now ram the gate."

"**What?** Are you crazy? I'm not going to ram the gate. It's not like it's plywood."

"This is a armored truck, for crissake. It's built like a tank."

Delvina leaned forward, mashed his foot down on the gas pedal, and the truck surged into the gate. There was a lot of noise and sparks and the gate buckled, snapping off its hinges.

With the exception of the private apartments, every inch of Rangeman is monitored, including the pavement outside the gate. When I decided to bring Delvina to Rangeman, I hadn't counted on ramming the gate. Now I was worried about not only getting shot by Delvina but by Ranger's Merry Men.

Snuggy and Doug were backed into a corner. Snuggy's eyes were wide, and Doug's eyes were narrowed. Delvina lumbered from the truck with the shotgun still leveled on me and ordered me to get out. I swung down just as Tank and Hal stepped out of the stairwell. They looked at me in cuffs, and they looked at Delvina with the shotgun, and the expression in their eyes was **oh shit!** The elevator doors opened and two more Rangeman guys stepped out with guns drawn.

Delvina opened his raincoat. "See this?" he said. "I'm wired to explode. I'm loaded with plastique. Shoot me, and this whole building goes. So drop your guns."

Everyone threw their guns on the floor, and Delvina looked around. "Where is he?"

"Who?" I asked.

"You know who. Diesel."

"He isn't here," Snuggy said. "Why have you got aluminum foil on your head?"

"It's so the horse don't talk to me."

Snuggy looked up at Doug. "You talk to him?"

Doug sort of shrugged. Or maybe it was just a muscle twitch in his shoulder.

"This isn't working out," Delvina said

to me, "and I'm getting real agitated. Every time you get involved in my business, it turns into a cluster fuck. I'll tell you what I'm gonna do. I'm gonna shoot you. And then I'm gonna shoot the horse. And then I'm gonna shoot all these guys in black. And then I'm gonna get the hell out of town." He scratched at his arm and at his neck. "Look at me. I'm itching again. It's the damn rash. I need more medicine."

"You can't shoot all of us with that shotgun," I said. "You can only shoot one of us."

"Yeah. I'm gonna shoot you with the shotgun. Then I'm gonna shoot everyone else with the Glock I got shoved in my pants."

"Ranger's gonna hate this," Tank said. "Better to get shot than to have to explain the gate. Bad enough I got a horse that smells like his shower gel."

I looked beyond Delvina and saw Diesel at the garage entrance.

"Hey, Delvina!" Diesel said. "Are you looking for me?"

Delvina turned to look at Diesel, and Doug lunged at Delvina, knocking him down. Tank and Hal rushed at Delvina and wrestled the guns from him.

"This isn't plastique taped to him," Tank said. "It's modeling clay."

"It was short notice," Delvina said. "I couldn't find any plastique."

Hal looked over at the armored truck. "Where'd that come from?"

"He borrowed it," I said.

Two police cars angled to a stop in front of the garage.

Diesel ambled over to me and released the handcuffs. "Are you okay?"

"Yep."

"Good thing I was here to rescue you."

Doug kicked Diesel in the leg, and Diesel went down to one knee.

"The horse says you're full of road apples," Delvina said to Diesel.

12

Lula pushed her way past the police. "Connie and me heard about this on the scanner, and we figured it had to be you," she said to me. "Where's Ranger? He still out of town?"

"Yep."

"I bet you can't wait to tell him how you drove a armored truck through his fancy-ass security gate."

Just thinking about it gave me creepy crawlies.

Delvina was going nuts in cuffs. "I itch everywhere," he said. "Someone scratch me. Scratch my nose. Am I breaking out? I need my medicine. I got a bottle in my pocket. Someone pop a pill in my mouth."

"I got big news," Lula said. "You'll never guess what came in the mail just now. Remember that photographer in Atlantic City? He sent me a letter. He said he was real sorry the photo shoot got moved, but he thought my pictures were hot, and he sold one of them to the tourist board, and they made it into a billboard. And he sent me this check for five thousand dollars and a picture of the billboard."

I looked at the photo. It was Lula in a red lace thong, and across her boobs was written WE CAN KEEP A SECRET IN ATLANTIC CITY—NO MATTER HOW BIG! Lula's left boob had to be about five feet wide on the billboard, and I couldn't even estimate the size of her ass.

"I gotta go to Atlantic City to see my billboard," Lula said. "This is so exciting. I know us supermodels aren't supposed to get excited about this shit, but I can't help it."

"Doug says he'd like to see your billboard, but we don't have a horse trailer anymore," Snuggy said.

"I talked it over with Stephanie's grandmother, and we've agreed that the Delvina money should go toward Doug's operation," Diesel said to Snuggy. "The money should more than cover the vet expenses and buy a horse trailer."

Snuggy's eyes got red and he swiped at his nose. "That's real nice of you. Doug says he's sorry he kicked you. And Doug just had a good idea. Maybe we can buy the RV from Grandma instead of a horse trailer, and then Doug and me can go on trips together."

"I'm sure Grandma would be happy to sell you the RV," I said.

"And I have more good news," Diesel said. "The issue with Doug's previous owner has been resolved, and Doug is officially in your care. I now pronounce you horse and leprechaun."

I walked outside with Diesel. "How did you know I was at Rangeman?"

"Lucky guess."

"I suppose this means you'll be moving on."

"Yeah, but I'll be back, Sweet Thing. Close your eyes and count to a hundred."

I counted to twenty and opened my eyes. Diesel was gone . . . and so was my bra.

About the Author

Janet Evanovich is the #1 bestselling author of the Stephanie Plum novels, twelve romance novels, the Alexandra Barnaby novels, and **How I Write: Secrets of a Bestselling Author.** She lives in New Hampshire and Florida.

LIKE WHAT YOU'VE SEEN?

If you enjoyed this large print edition of
PLUM LUCKY, here are a few of Janet Evanovich's
latest bestsellers also available in large print.

LEAN MEAN THIRTEEN
(hardcover)
978-0-7393-2733-3 • 0-7393-2733-X
$29.95/$37.95C

PLUM LOVIN'
(hardcover)
978-0-375-43204-0 • 0-375-43204-3
$22.95/$29.95C

TWELVE SHARP
(hardcover)
978-0-7393-2643-5 • 0-7393-2643-0
$28.95/$38.95C

ELEVEN ON TOP
(hardcover)
978-0-375-43533-1 • 0-375-43533-6
$28.95/$42.00C

Large print books are available wherever books
are sold and at many local libraries.

All prices are subject to change. Check with your
local retailer for current pricing and availability.
For more information on these and other large print titles,
visit www.randomhouse.com/largeprint.